The Bucket List

Lee Somheil

Copyright © 2018 Lee Somheil

All rights reserved.

ISBN: 1718909446
ISBN-13: 978-1718909441

For all the Leesies of the world.

THE BUCKET LIST

- ☐ Complete everything on my bucket list
- ☐ Write a letter to Harry ♡
- ☐ Pose as a college student
- ☐ Go skydiving
- ☐ Go on a date with Jesse
- ☐ Watch all the Twilight movies in one day
- ☐ Party all night long
- ☐ Go zip-lining
- ☐ Dance under the stars
- ☐ Write a song
- ☐ Have a paint fight
- ☐ Stand under the Hollywood sign
- ☐ Go to the top of the Eiffel Tower
- ☐ Go shopping in New York
- ☐ Kiss a British guy
- ☐ Learn to surf
- ☐ Sleep under the stars
- ☐ Cuddle under fireworks
- ☐ Shop at the Mall of America
- ☐ Learn to play piano
- ☐ Work at Hollister
- ☐ Build a treehouse
- ☐ Play hide and seek in Ikea
- ☐ Get my cartilage pierced
- ☐ Bake in the middle of the night
- ☐ Fly first class
- ☐ Find my perfect dress
- ☐ Go goth for a day
- ☐ Sing in front of a crowd

The cold metal chair was rock-hard, and I had been sitting in it for ages. I just really, really wanted to go to bed, where I could give in to the sadness, and perhaps finally clear the giant lump in my throat.

After what felt like hours of waiting, a smoky-haired officer sauntered into the interrogation room and sat across the table from me. "Hi, Elise. I'm Detective Harlem." I almost laughed that such a stereotypical old white cop had the last name "Harlem." But I wasn't exactly in the mood for laughing. With everything that had happened, combined with him calling me "Elise," my first impression of Detective Harlem wasn't great.

I waited a few seconds before answering, allowing the mood to incubate. "I go by Leesie."

Harlem sighed, then threw his first procedural question at me. "When did you last see Tate?"

"Day before yesterday." My voice was void of emotion.

The Detective nodded, as if I hadn't already told seven people and an orange form that. "Was she acting strange?"

I stared at him for a second, incredulously. "I mean, she was depressed..."

"Did she say anything to you, involving the possibility of suicide or self-harm?"

I scoffed. "She's barely talked to me in the last three months, so no."

"But I thought you were best friends."

"We were."

"Then why did you stop talking?" he pressed.

"No clue," I answered sassily, irritated with his barrage of questions.

"Do you know of any people she would've confided in?"

I shrugged. "Tate and I had different friends."

After squinting at me for several moments, Harlem stood up abruptly. "I'm sorry for your loss, Elise. You're free to go. We'll contact you if we need to speak with you further."

Although he tried to hide it, it was apparent that he didn't care. He had better things to do than to deal with me, the moody teenager. They all did.

I flashed him the dryest smile I could muster, then proceeded to push the chair away from the table. The legs scraped ruthlessly against the dull tiled floor, filling the silent room with a disgusting noise. I stood up, not bothering to push the chair back in. What did it matter?

I left the interrogation room without looking back, and let the door slam behind me. I trudged past police officers typing on computers, filling out paperwork, or casually reading the newspaper at their desks. In the corner, a coffee maker beeped and steamed, as the smell of the coffee drifted throughout the room.

The entire atmosphere felt so warm, so friendly, that it made me feel sick. How could they be so happy?

I kept walking until I reached the spot where my mom was having a pity conversation with the receptionist. I stood by her side, but the two women wouldn't stop talking, and eventually I couldn't take it any longer.

"I'm going to wait outside," I muttered, before leaving the station through the glass doors.

Outside, I couldn't help but notice the absolute silence. Shielding my eyes from the bright sun, I could see cheerful people walking past on the sidewalk, but the noise of their conversations failed to cross the void between us. Nearby, several birds sat on an electrical wire, but no noise escaped their beaks. No noise could bleed through the hot humid air. No noise could enter my breaking heart.

    Throughout that day, and the coming weeks, there was one thought persistently echoing in my mind: *Why'd she do it?* My life seemed nearly identical to Tate's, yet I couldn't fathom choosing to die.
Tate and I were best friends for twelve years. How had I not known what was going to happen?
    During the first few weeks after Tate died, people left and right turned to me hoping for answers. And I didn't have any answers.
    Day after day, I'd sit in the swivel chair at my weak white desk, while thoughts trampled through my head like elephants. I'd try to decipher any meaning from my last conversations with Tate, try to figure out ways I could've stopped what happened, try so hard to find someone, anyone, to blame. For weeks after the suicide, I didn't do anything else.
    Every morning, light would seep through my window, illuminating the putrid pink bedroom walls. I'd drag myself out of bed and into the desk chair, and then I'd sit there while the tears got old. I was alone. Tate had shut my door; grief had locked it.
    I'd spend the days hunched in my swivel chair, resting my head on the cool surface of the desk. All the while, I'd stare at the empty lines of a blank piece of notebook paper, wondering what words I could fill the page with.
    My mom had come up with the brilliant idea that I should pour my soul out onto the paper, as some sort of therapeutic coping method. I'm sure she expected me to come downstairs an hour later, with a melancholy smile, and say "I'm moving on, Mom." Yeah, well tough.
    I did try. I wanted to write, but I couldn't bring myself to do it. Time and time again, I'd wearily force my fingers to curl around the purple pom-pom pen laying next to the paper. I tried to tell my hand to bring the tip to the paper, but would always feel too weak, fresh out of motivation to put in some effort and help myself. Then I'd

give in, release the pen, and hear the all-too-familiar noise of it clattering against the wooden surface of the desk.

That became my life: sitting there, a lonely sack of sadness, contemplating the same things again and again and again.

Every weekday after the suicide, my parents would visit me up in my pity pit and ask me if I wanted to go to school, and I'd always say no. Then I'd sit in my desk chair for the rest of the day, until darkness fell and I collapsed on my bed for yet another sleepless night.

Two weeks passed, and besides going after-hours to take finals, I hadn't gone to school once. It had been sixteen days since I'd talked to any of my friends. I knew that eventually, some little distraction would wander into my life and keep me busy for a while, but not for long. There was no getting over this.

A distraction arrived on the third of June, two days after school ended. I had officially graduated high school, but hadn't given that any real thought yet.

I was sitting in the chair, as usual, when my mom came into my room, holding the phone. "Leesie, it's Maddie." Hesitantly, I took the phone from her. Maddie was Tate's mom.

"Hello?"

"Hi, Leesie." Maddie chirped in her usual cheerful tone, but I could tell it was completely faked. "So, I'm, um... I'm cleaning out some of," Maddie paused and took a breath, "I'm cleaning out some of Tate's things. So, if you want anything... stop on by and help yourself."

"Okay," I replied with such hesitance it emerged as a whisper. My voice was weak from not being used. "I'll think about it."

I pressed the end button on the phone, and slowly raised my gaze up to my mom, who was still standing there with a look of vague concern and reluctant curiosity.

"Why was she calling?" she coaxed, sugar coating her words with a nice, sweet, happy glaze.

I responded quietly, "She invited me to go over there and... help her clean out, or something." The second I let the words escape my lips, I knew my mom would force me to go. I could've lied, but I'm definitely not the type that lies to their parents.

"Sweetheart," she crouched down to my eye level, "you should go." I was about to protest, when she continued, "It's what Tate would've wanted."

A burst of adrenaline and fury rushed through my veins. How would she know what Tate would've wanted? My mom barely knew Tate; what gave her the right to make me feel guilty? But I remained silent, and tore my eyes away from her's so she wouldn't see my lividity.

"Alright," I muttered. "Okay."

I raised my fist up to the light green door, then let my knuckles fall against it in a half-hearted knock. I'd stood on that step a thousand times, and when Maddie opened up, I wondered if that would be the last time I'd ever stand there again.

"Hey, Leesie." She gave a weak smile, then hugged me softly. It was a we've-shared-a-tragedy-hug, so I hugged back in the same way. She pulled away, and whispered, "I've cleaned out most of the house. You..." She paused suddenly, choking up. "You can do her room. I... I can't go in there." Then she walked briskly away, turned a corner, and was out of sight. I was alone.

I knew Tate's house exceptionally well, arguably better than my own. I took a minute to peer around, reminiscing in the past that would no longer be my future. I stared at the loft where Tate and I had played make-believe, sometimes for the entire day.

My eyes scanned the living room, then fell on the cramped study opposite from me. Sometimes, when we were feeling lazy, we'd sit in there playing Zoo Tycoon and trap the guests in the cages. We would laugh and laugh at that.

Glancing through the open door, I noticed the silhouette of a person sitting at the desk. It took me a moment to recognize it as Tate's father. He didn't look like himself, with his shoulders sagging and his head bent down. Seeing him like that caused a feeling of despair to settle over my heart. He was usually so strong.

I stared at him for a minute, waiting for him to show any sign of life, but he didn't even twitch. He reminded me vaguely of myself, spending hours sitting in the desk chair without the will to do anything, even move. We shared the same hell.

Shaking myself out of my trance, I took off my shoes and laid them on a toddler-sized wooden chair that was by the door. That's not where shoes were supposed to go, but I'd been putting mine there for as long as I can remember.

I began hiking up the silky, white, carpeted stairway. Once I reached the top and walked to Tate's door, I took a deep breath. This was it. I exhaled and twisted the doorknob.

I don't know what I was expecting, but I was shocked when I trooped inside. It was... untouched. Normal. As if nothing had changed. It made me irritated, seeing her bedroom like that, as happy and colorful as ever. It was as if it was lying to the world, hiding what had happened.

Not only did it seem normal, it seemed busy. There were papers scattered about on Tate's desk, math homework and an unfinished english project. Nothing about what became of her. No "Dear World" or, "To My Best Friend" letters.

I scavenged around, not finding too much I wanted to keep. I took a couple of Tate's favorite books, and a fashion magazine or two. There was an old bucket list I found in her closet, which I'm sure she hadn't even seen for months, but I decided to take that too. Some memories are too hard to leave behind.

The summer right before high school was probably when we were closest. We were excited for our big transition to a new school, to meet new people, to make new friends, but stick by each other no matter what. Well, that was flushed down the drain.

One summer's afternoon while we were sitting on Tate's bedroom floor, she had this idea that we should make bucket lists. Everything we wanted to do in our lives, written down in one easy-to-use checklist. I gave up after five minutes, but Tate worked on her's for days.

I didn't want a bucket list. Why would I? I was happy with my life just the way it was. I figured Tate and I would do great things someday, but unlike her, I had no idea what those things were going to be. So I decided to let her make the list, and I'd follow along.

Looking back, I realize Tate was never content with her life. She was happy, don't get me wrong, but not content. There was always something she wanted or somewhere she wished she was, besides what she had and where she happened to be.

Bringing myself back down to earth, I picked up Tate's alarm clock. It made a cute fountain of water spurt out and played surfing songs when it was time to wake up. I loved that thing; it used to make me so jealous. When I picked it up, I saw that all of the water had evaporated. I placed it in the box, then had a seat on her bed.

I set the box aside and reached for her lime green pillow. It was a birthday present from me, years ago. I wondered if she still remembered that, or if it was just another pillow taking up space. Then I realized that the last person to be on Tate's bed was probably Tate, which made my chest hurt really badly.

I picked up the cardboard box and quickly walked out of the room, shutting the door behind me. It stung that everything that I had left of Tate I could hold in my arms. It was never supposed to end that way. Actually, it was never supposed to end.

Before leaving, I exchanged glances with Maddie, who once again gave a weak smile and a pathetic little wave.

Once I was back home I immediately climbed up the stairs to my room. I took out the books and stored them away on my bookshelf, perhaps to be read in the future. I threw my old alarm clock into the back of my closet and replaced it with Tate's, smiling once I saw how it looked with everything else in the room. I didn't know where to put the bucket list, so I just set it on my desk. I decided I'd find a place for it later.

THE BUCKET LIST

Drained, I fell down onto my bed, and simply lay there. So this was my life now. This was what I was: forsaken, forgotten, and futile.

Time passed, as it always does, and I stayed in bed, aware of it's passing, but not interacting with it. A day or two after I went to Tate's house, I was curled up on my bed when I heard a knock at my bedroom door.

"Yeah?" I called to the knocker. My mom dawdled up every once in a while to offer me some soup or tea, which I was in the habit of refusing.

"Can I come in?" a low voice requested.

I sat up instantly. "Jesse?" Jesse slowly pushed the door open and peeked inside.

"Hey," he said. Jesse was Tate's friend. He'd always been Tate's friend, since before I knew her.

What I primarily wanted to know was why Jesse was at my house, unannounced. I decided it would be rude to ask, though, so instead I said, "Hi."

"How are you?" he inquired in a concerned tone.

I raised one eyebrow, and lied. "Fine. You?"

He nodded, and didn't answer for a minute. "I'm okay."

"Good," I answered.

An awkward silence ensued. I perched on the edge of my bed and Jesse stood near the door, leaning towards it as if he would be leaving at any second. But, alas, to no avail. Jesse turned and strolled across my room. He peered at the bucket list, and chuckled as he read number four: "Go on a date with Jesse." Finally, he clarified, "This was Tate's?"

"Uh, yeah. I went over to her house the other day, and picked up a few things."

Jesse turned and fixed me with an intense gaze, that I quite desperately wanted to look away from, but I resisted the urge. "Yeah? Maddie called me, but I wasn't feeling exactly... up to it."

I nodded. "Mmm hmm."

Turning back to the list, he said, "Well, it's cool. Are you going to try and finish it?" He sounded interested, almost excited.

"Um, no."

He took a step back toward the door. "Oh, no, of course not. My bad."

"I mean, it's not mine…"

"I know, I know. I get it." He fidgeted with his hands, then ran them through his black hair.

I bit my lip. I didn't know what to say.

"Well… I should get going. It was nice seeing you."

"Bye."

Once his footsteps had faded, I collapsed face first onto my pillow. Talking to Jesse always made me want to scream in frustration.

The trouble started when he asked me to a dance in eighth grade. On one hand, Jesse was nice and sweet and cute and way out of my league. But, on the other hand, Tate was practically in love with him, which meant that he was off-limits for me. Naturally, I rejected him, but it made it incredibly awkward whenever we saw each other, especially when Tate wasn't around. I never told Tate, and I don't think Jesse did either, but somehow she still knew that he had a crush on me.

Plus, I'd always felt like I was competing with Jesse for Tate. I felt guilty for stealing away his best friend.

And why would he suggest that I finish the bucket list? I mean, it was Tate's, not mine. If I completed the list, it would be like taking it away from her. Wouldn't it?

I added the bucket list to things I tried not to think about, along with belts and everything else that had to do with Tate. It really sucks when thinking about your best friend makes you sad. That's the opposite of what best friends are for. Yet there I was.

It bugged me that Jesse was so excited about the bucket list. If Tate had wanted to finish it, she would've. She didn't need me to uphold her legacy or whatever. But I couldn't stop thinking about the list, and the day that Tate first wrote it.

I missed that Tate, the Tate that would jot down her life ambitions on a little piece paper. She was fun. She was happy. She was alive. I'm not sure what it was, but something caused her to go downhill after that summer. Maybe high school was too much for her. Or maybe the depression was entirely random.

That's what continued to haunt me. Above all, it wasn't my loss that I dwelled on, it was that Tate went without a single word or clue, she was just gone. What was killing me was not knowing what killed her.

☐ WRITE A LETTER TO HARRY ♡

One Saturday at 5:57 (yes, A.M.), my dad burst into my room with such noise and gusto I nearly fell out of bed. "Leesie! The sun is shining, the birds are singing. Let's do something great!"

I managed to let out some nonsensical noise, which my dad took as encouragement.

"What do you want to wear today? A dress? Overalls?" He walked over to my dresser and began opening drawers.

"Dad..." I managed to groan.

"Okay, okay," he relented. "I'll be downstairs making pancakes. I expect you down there in five minutes or I'll be back up here to drag you down!"

Yeah, my dad was being super annoying and giving me a headache, but I had to hand it to him, it was nice to see how hard he was trying. He clearly just wanted me to have fun, be a teenager, and wear overalls. It must hurt to have your daughter sitting behind a closed door all day, every day, crying and thinking about death. So, I decided to eat some pancakes, more for his sake than mine. Also, my dad makes fantastic pancakes.

I dug to the back of my closet until I found a blue sundress that I hadn't worn for years, and pulled it on. I figured it would make my dad happy.

I trampled down the stairs half asleep. Luckily, when I reached the kitchen, someone put pancakes and coffee in front of me, which made me feel much better about being awake before the sun had even set in China.

"So good to see you down here, Leesie," my mother cooed. I seriously considered using my pancakes as a pillow, then decided not to, mostly because of the grossness factor.

When I made it back upstairs, I sprawled out on my bed, but my restlessness held me back from the luxury of sleep. Finally, I decided I should actually do something for a change. The problem was, I didn't know what that something should be.

I glanced over at Tate's bucket list, which was still sitting unassumingly on my desk. I chuckled. There were a few cute things thrown in to Tate's ultimately serious list. The first item was to write a letter to Harry Styles from One Direction.

I wasn't a huge admirer of the band. Don't get me wrong, I would listen to their songs every once in a while, and be there for Tate when she needed someone to fangirl to, but I was never a diehard fan. Tate was a different story. She was a full-fledged Directioner.

I was abruptly pulled out of my thoughts when my phone buzzed on my desk. I jolted, and immediately grabbed it to see who had texted me. The notification read, "One new message from Jess!"

It had been almost a week since anyone had messaged me. Right off the bat, I was getting texts left and right. Nearly half of the human population was trying to make me believe they were a puddle of tears over my loss. I never sent anything back, and after a while, they took the hint and gave up. So of course I was expecting some emotional, meaningful message topped off with a Mark Twain quote from Jesse, just like all of the others. I opened the text.

Jess: *hey*

Oh great, he was hoping for a full on therapy session. Talk about emotions and feelings, bring up sad and happy memories, I think not.

I dropped my phone back onto the desk. Even if I was searching to talk out my sadness, which I wasn't, I wouldn't want to talk it out with Jesse. He wasn't exactly, well, serious. He'd try to be funny, all of the time. He'd try to sway the conversation in his direction to get a chuckle out of people, and he was charming but he wasn't deep. Maybe that's why we'd stopped being friends: I finally realized he was too single layered for my liking.

I thought back to our conversation from a few days before, which weirded me out a little bit. I mean, I guess it made sense. We were both Tate's friends. But it seemed so bizarre for him to actually come over solely for the purpose of having a brief talk. And about what, really?

I suddenly turned back to the bucket list, and thought about what he'd asked: "Are you going to try and complete it?" Why would he bring that up? I mean, that's weird, right?

Ugh, I was over-analyzing yet again. Sometimes I'd rethink something over and over before I could make any sense out of it. I tried to stop thinking through the conversation with Jesse, but it was one of the only safe things for me to mull over.

"Leesie?" my mom's voice called faintly from downstairs.

I groaned, pushing myself out of the chair and opening the door. "Yeah?" I yelled back.

"Oh, you're back in your room..." she muttered, as if she expected me to be somewhere else. I heard her stepping up the carpeted stairs, heading toward me. "Leesie, I want to ask you something."

There are only a few types of fear in this life, and "I want to ask you something" is one of them. "Yeah?"

She sighed, then ambled through the door and slowly lowered herself to the edge of my bed. Staring at me both sympathetically and sternly, she patted the spot next to her until I sat down. "Leesie, sweetie, I think we should go see a therapist. Just, you know, talk. I ran into Maddie earlier and she suggested a great lady."

"Mom, please... I'm fine. Don't make me."

She examined me with that worried-mother expression. "Please go, honey, just once? Try it out?"

I rolled my eyes. On one hand, it sounded awful, but on the other hand, my mom was giving me those puppy-dog eyes. Maybe it would give her a glimmer of hope. Maybe her having hope would give me hope too. So I relented.

I was shocked at how quickly my mom was able to get me an appointment. Apparently, the therapist knew Maddie well, so she scheduled us for the very next day. Which meant I had to shower, which meant I had to get up before noon, a rare occurance for me since Tate's death.

That morning, I slumped down the stairs. My brightly grinning mother stood waiting for me at the door, dressed absurdly business-like and holding a large stack of papers.

"We've got a little paperwork to fill out; you can do it in the car." She smiled and handed the papers to me. She looked as though she was telling me that we'd be getting frozen yogurt on the way, not that I had lots of tedious work to do.

Eventually, I ended up in a cushy gray chair, in the lobby of a large office building. A few minutes passed, and as they did, I started feeling more and more doubtful that anything would come of the therapy.

Before long, a tall, skinny, brown-haired lady in impossibly high stilettos appeared from around the corner.

"Hi, Sarah and Leesie, I'm Dr. Señuarez. How are you?" Dr. Señuarez-- what a therapist's name.

"Hi. I'm good. How are you?" My mom beamed at her.

"Good! So, let's get started!" She led us down an awkwardly long hallway, to the furthest reaches of the apparently quite expansive building. Once we reached the far end of the hall, we turned right and entered a cramped room. Inside, there were two brown armchairs and a large black couch, topped off with a lovely painting of a forest and a waterfall that made me reach into my soul and find my inner self.

I sat on the couch, resisting the urge to kick back and relax. My mother and the therapist took the two brown chairs. We talked for a while, about what had happened, our family, money, college, and so on.

Eventually, Dr. Señuarez turned to my mom and said, "Alright, now I should get to know Leesie a bit, one on one. You can wait in the lobby; she'll be out soon!" The therapist radiated so much fake optimism, it was like she was wearing makeup on her personality.

"Oh, uh... okay," my mom said, as if she hadn't expected to be sent away. "See you, Leesie!" She took her purse and walked out. And right as the door shut, the makeup came off.

"I want to be real Leesie. What happened to you was rough. I knew Tate myself, and she was an amazing girl."

"Oh, you knew her?" I asked, surprised.

Dr. Señuarez nodded, then subsequently changed the topic. "So how about you and I push that aside for now. I don't want to pressure you to spill your thoughts and feelings to me before you're ready."

I was confused. (Wasn't that the point of a therapist?) "What do you mean, Dr. Señuarez?"

"A conversation is a road, it can be long and twisty turny, but continue on long enough and it connects you to every other road in the country. It'll come up when it comes up. And call me Jenni, I only use the title to charm the parents." She grinned, exposing her pristine white teeth. On second thought, maybe this woman wasn't so bad. She seemed insightful, yet young enough that I could relate to her.

"Okay..."

"What's really important," Jenni continued, "is that you realize you'll eventually have to move on with your life. Do the things you've always wanted to do, and don't let Tate's death ruin you."

I remained silent, staring at her.

"What do you want to do in your life, Leesie?" she pressed. Once again, I remained silent. "Do you have any... dreams? Goals?"

I didn't respond, and merely mumbled incoherently and scrutinized my hands.

"It doesn't have to be goals. I don't know, maybe just some fun things you've always wanted to do. Can you think of anything?"

"You mean, like, a bucket list?" I suggested before I could stop myself.

Jenni perked up. "There we go, yeah. You have a bucket list?"

I made eye contact with her for the first time since my mom left. My thoughts were fireworks going off across a dark mind. Finally, I muttered, "Yeah."

"Nice! Maybe you could try to cross something off that list, to take your mind away from things?"

"Yeah," I echoed. What was I doing?

"Leesie, I'm a strong believer that we should quit while we're ahead. Go home, take a look at the list, maybe knock one thing off in your free time. We can talk more about it when you see me next!" When you see me next? Mom had already planned another visit, hadn't she?

"So, that was nice, wasn't it?" my mom piped cheerfully in the car on the way home.

I somberly placed my forehead in my hand. "It was fine, Mom, but I don't want to go back. I don't need it."

"Well, if I see you improve and learn from what Dr. Señuarez taught us, you don't have to go back."

"But Mom!" I whined. "That wasn't the deal!"

"It's what's best for you." That shut me up, although I didn't see how spending tons of money to have a chat with a stranger was good for me.

The next day, I decided I should do something productive to prevent going back. Also, I didn't want to leave Tate's bucket list on my desk forever, where it would do nothing but take up space and make me miss her even more.

And therefore, I ended up back at my desk, with the bucket list lying in front of me. Before I could begin to think about what I was going to do, my phone buzzed again. Another text from "Jess." I sighed, and unlocked the phone.

Jess: *Leesie??*

I felt a tinge of guilty for ignoring to his last text, but I didn't know what to say.

Me: *what*

I'd been giving a lot of people the cold shoulder recently, so I hardly noticed my rudeness.

I went back to thinking. I picked up the list, and scanned it. There weren't too many things listed that I could easily accomplish that day, unfortunately, but the first item was to write a letter to Harry Styles, which seemed easy enough. I wouldn't write a letter to One Direction under normal circumstances, especially not to Harry. As cute as he was, he was probably my least favorite. But Tate had always had a thing for him, so I wanted to make it as good as possible.

Dear Harry, I wrote, and was immediately interrupted by my phone buzzing again.

Jess: *How are you doing?*

Me: *You already asked me that when you decided to show up at my doorstep*

I just wanted to write the letter. I turned my phone from vibrate to silent; whatever he had to say could wait until I had at least one thing checked off the list.

I reread the letter, contemplating what to write next. After writing some, then erasing some, writing some more, etc., I had a finished copy.

Dear Harry,

Hi. My name's Leesie. I'm eighteen years old, and just finished being a senior at Batavia Lake. Not that you've heard of that, it's some American high school far across the pond in the middle of Illinois. Do British people really say that?

Honestly, I'm not writing this letter because I'm a diehard fan. Let's just say I'm writing it for a friend. But I do like your music. It's nice. There's a lot of lovey dovey, though.

Blah blah blah. The letter droned on with more random facts and uninterest. I folded it up, mumbled a quick prayer for Harry, who'd have to read it, slid it into an envelope and wrote the address of One Direction's public mail box. I put it on my desk to put in the mailbox later. Unfortunately, my proactivity had been spent; I was officially too lazy to finish the job.

I plopped down on my bed, then unlocked my phone and saw that there was yet another text from Jesse.

Jess: *I just wanted you to know that you can talk to me about it*

Oh God. I'd heard that from about every person I knew. And some I didn't.

Jess: *I'm going through the same thing.*

I was slightly taken aback. Nobody was closer to Tate than I was, even though Jesse had known her longer. While his bond with Tate had been strong, it was nothing compared to what I'd had with her.

Me: *i know*

I didn't want to talk. Not to him, not to anyone. I already saw that therapist; I didn't need another. I sighed and threw my phone down on my end table. It clattered pathetically before falling motionless, awaiting another message from someone else trying to care. My eyelids felt heavy. I wasn't sleepy tired, but I just couldn't put up with being awake any longer. And so I slept.

☑ Write a letter to Harry ♡

☐ POSE AS A COLLEGE STUDENT

I woke up at 7:05 in the evening to the sound of rain. I wasn't groggy; I felt refreshed. I had a strange urge in me, an urge to do something. That was new.

After a few moments of thought, I decided putting some earbuds in and listening to music was something enough, so I rummaged through my drawer and pulled out my little iPod Shuffle. My iPhone had the exact same music on it, but I felt entranced by the concept of a Shuffle. Not knowing what would play, letting it remain a mystery until the song began, captivated me. I don't know, maybe I was a weirdo.

The first song to play was "Back Home" by Andy Grammer. I had a love-hate relationship with that song; on the one hand, it was upbeat and happy, but it made me miss Tate, because we first heard it together.

Before the first verse had finished, I had already started crying. I blamed the weather, but deep down I knew the rain wasn't to blame. I hopelessly missed Tate. How could I not? She was the only person who knew me for who I truly was. With everyone else it felt as if I was wearing some sort of mask. Or perhaps like the therapist, I'd applied layers upon layers of makeup onto my personality.

I hastily commanded myself to snap out of it. I was thinking about her again. And that never led anywhere good.

I wanted to move on from Tate, of course I did. But I didn't know how. I didn't know if I could. And I knew that, realistically, it would be years before I could go even a single day without thinking about Tate. I had years, though, and that was the important thing. I knew I could move on, eventually.

Amid the crying and thinking, I heard my phone buzz. I sighed out loud. It was, of course, a text from Jesse.

Jess: *wanna hang out tomorrow?*

"Wanna hang out?" Wanna hang out?! Of all the things I needed to see at that moment, that was most definitely the very last. Here I was, little more than a sobbing ball of tears, and Jesse wanted to "hang out?" What did that even mean?

I typed back a message telling him to leave me alone, but I stopped myself before I sent it. I decided to simply ignore him, at least for a bit, until I calmed down.

When I was done with my little waterworks show, I decided I should probably text him back. But the problem with, "Wanna hang out?" is that it's impossible to say no or that you can't without A. lying, or B. sounding mean. Plus, maybe he was going through the same thing, and maybe he was just after a little two-way consolation.

So, what happened happened.

Me: *sure.*

The car door slammed shut, and I waved at my mom through the window. Tilting my head back, I peered up at the expansive building that read *Northern Illinois University* along the top. I was at the college because of the bucket list; impersonating a college student was the next task. I was supposed to be hanging out with Jesse today, but he had yet to text me. So for now, I was here.

I began wandering around the campus, stopping here and there to check out the interior of a building or investigate an outdoor spot. It was morning, about ten, so lots of students were around, rushing to their next class or studying on the faded lawn.

I was surprised by the amount of people around, considering the time of year. I suppose the bustling students were taking summer classes, and the more relaxed ones simply staying a few extra weeks before heading home for break. And then, of course, there was me, a heartbroken girl pretending to be a college student solely because it was on her dead friend's bucket list.

Eventually, I settled on the front steps of a building that, according to the sign posted next to it, was the astronomy hall. I removed my phone from my pocket, saw that I didn't have any new texts, and started playing some games on my phone. I don't know, what else was there to do?

About half a minute after I sat down, I was pulled away from my phone when a cute blond guy sat next to me. "Hey."

I smiled at him. "Hi."

He pulled a thick textbook out of his backpack. I read the cover: *Economics 101*.

I sighed. I had had to take economics at my school last year. "Ahh, Econ..."

The boy rolled his shimmering blue eyes. "I know, right? Do you have Jerkowski?"

Suddenly, I realized that I had dug myself into quite a deep hole. I had to keep my cover, so I lied. "Yeah."

"He's the worst, isn't he?"

"Well yeah, and it doesn't help that the material is so boring."

He studied me for a moment too long, then held out his hand. "I'm Asher. Architecture major. You?"

I grabbed his hand and shook it. "Leesie, and I'm studying, um..." I paused. "English."

"Whoa. Bet your parents are thrilled with that choice."

I shrugged. "Devastated, actually, but whatever."

He gazed at me for an extended moment once again. "Want to go get lunch?" he finally offered.

I nodded. "Sure."

When we arrived at the building that evidently served as the cafeteria, I let Asher lead the way inside. There was a man standing by a cash register when we entered, and Asher handed him what appeared to be a credit card.

"Student I.D. please," the beefy security dude requested.

"I, uh... dang it, I forgot it in my dorm!"

"Don't worry, I got you." Asher handed his card to the guy again, and he swiped it for me.

"Thanks!"

We sat down side by side at a table near an immense window. The table was meant for eight people, but we were the only two there.

I sat there, awkwardly and silently, as did he. He appeared to be a bit confused, and I suddenly felt nervous. Was I supposed to be doing something?

"You going to..." he trailed off, with wonder in his voice.

"What?" I asked sincerely.

"We going to go get food?" he questioned with scrunched eyebrows.

"Oh yeah! 'Course! Yup, I was just uh, waiting for you to say the word!" I answered rapidly and nervously.

"Right..." he trailed off, then got up and led the way.

Let me tell you: college is the life. The food was amazing and... well, the food was amazing, and frankly that did it for me.

When we were finished with a delightful and awkward meal, we tossed our trash, and Asher offered to walk me to German (which I told him I was going to next).

"It doesn't start for a while. I think I'm going to go back to my dorm; I forgot something," I told him.

"Oh, well alright." He shrugged. "So, you wanna hang out, or something? You know, like, whenever?"

Wow. I was being asked out by a cute college boy. I decided I should probably stop pretending to be a student there. "Uh... sorry, but I have a boyfriend."

Needless to say, Asher was a bit surprised. So was I. A short uncomfortable silence ensued, but it felt to me as though it lasted at least half of an hour. It was interrupted when my phone buzzed in my pocket. I pulled it out and glanced at the lock screen. The notification read, "One new message from Jess!"

I peered up at Asher, and tried to work through the awkwardness. "I should probably get going."

"Oh, well, okay." He managed to smile. "I'll see you around then. Bye!"

I speedily walked away, feeling his eyes drilling into my back. Once I was safely outside, I erupted into a fit of laughter. I imagined what Tate would've said had she been there. It would've made the whole thing funnier by tenfold. I can remember countless times when we were both slap happy, laughing until we were crying.

All of a sudden, I had a realization. I stopped laughing dead in my tracks, and had to sit down on the curb. I realized that Tate would've loved to finish her bucket list. Maybe not recent Tate, but fourteen-year-old Tate. And she would've loved the idea of me completing it after her tragic death. She was sentimental that way. So I was stuck then; I had to do it.

☑ Pose as a college student

☐ GO SKYDIVING

After my mom picked me up, I asked her to take me to Jesse's house. During the dull car ride, I decided to finally open some of my pity texts.

The first message was from my friend Rose, who I'd chatted up back in Political Science junior year. It was a list of sentimental quotes, separated by squiggly dashes and topped off with a "I hope you get better soon!"

Another was from my Uncle Jim, who had sent something like eight paragraphs worth of text. He was a writer, and it quite obviously showed. I didn't even try reading that one.

Finally, I scrolled through my messages looking to open a third, without much hope of anything worth reading. I picked one from my friend Ella.

Ella: *Hey. How are you?*

Now that was unexpected. It was so normal, so relaxed. It was refreshing.

That had always been the great thing about Ella: she was chill. On the day we met, I had been freaking out. I didn't know where my classes were, I forgot my locker combo something like four times, and I couldn't stop saying the dumbest things to my classmates. But she was totally calm, as if the first day of high school was no big deal. I had walked up to my locker to see her standing at her's next door, putting books in like it was a completely normal day.

Thinking about that day, I realized how nerve-racking skydiving, the next thing on the list, would be. Maybe Ella could come, and her calmness would rub off on me again.

I texted her back, asking if she was interested. She responded quickly, saying that her parents probably wouldn't let her, but she would try her best to convince them. Which got me thinking: how was I going to convince my parents?

I pushed that out of my mind for the time being, because I had a more immediate problem on my hands. And that problem was Jesse.

I stepped up onto his front porch and jammed at the button by the door with my finger. A high-pitched bell rung through his massive house. I used to go over to Jesse's place at least once a week, but standing there, it felt unfamiliar.

The door opened almost immediately, which frankly creeped me out, to reveal Jesse wearing a casual Blackhawks hoodie. "Hey, Leesie!" he greeted me with a grin, and suddenly it was as if no time had passed. As if that Jesse was the same Jesse I had been friends with years ago. Maybe it was.

I almost hugged him, I even quickly stepped forward as if I was going to, but I stopped before I could break through the unyielding walls that four years had put between us. I took a deep breath, reminded myself about the years that had passed, and tried to accept that he wasn't the same. I tried to accept that I wasn't either.

I forced a smile onto my face. "Hi," I responded. "What's up?"

"Graham and I were just eating some pizza. Come on, have a piece." He led the way into his kitchen, where his younger brother was sitting at the table. Graham was two years younger than us, and though we'd never deliberately excluded him, Tate, Jesse, and I had always found him annoying.

Jesse shoved a semi-warm piece of pizza into my unsuspecting hands, forcing me to accept it. "Pepperoni, your favorite." He winked at me. I managed a chuckle. It was weird that he remembered that from, like, seventh grade.

"So..." I began. Before I could get any further, he took my arm and dragged me upstairs, into the loft. We sat down on his black leather couch, facing the colossal flat screen that they'd had for years.

We started talking about this and that. Every once in a while we would turn to the TV to watch whatever was on, but most of the time the speaker's noise remained in the background. As we chatted, the conversation went from small talk to a discussion of things I actually found interesting.

"So, I went to NIU today," I told him.

"What? Why?"

I shrugged. "For fun."

He inspected my expression, proceeding to raise his eyebrows. "I don't believe you. If I have one talent in this world, it's knowing when Leesie Derell is lying."

I snickered. It was true, Jesse was unspeakably good at suspecting when I was bending the truth. I avoided making eye contact, and focused my attention on the TV.

"Hmm..." he murmured, deep in thought. "You've been working on the bucket list, haven't you? I remember something about a college on there."

When a guilty look began spreading across my face, he added, "You scoundrel!"

This surprised me enough that I turned to face him. "What?"

"You should've included me. It was my idea to work on the list, after all."

I bit my lip. "Well..." I didn't really know how to continue. Jesse crossed his arms in a fake-anger sort of way.

I thought for a minute, then decided, *why not?* "I do need someone to go skydiving with. If you think you could convince your parents?"

He perked back up, becoming cheerful again. "Anything for Tate."

My strategy was simple: a house divided cannot stand. I targeted my dad first, since he was the easy kill. Then I could use him to take down my mom.

I found him alone in the kitchen that evening. Our conversation started with me saying, "Hey, Dad," in that cute little girl voice that no father could resist from their daughter.

"Hi, sweetie," he replied, leaning against the kitchen counter.

"So, I've been thinking," I started.

"Have you?" he asked, as though that was a surprise.

I rolled my eyes. "Anyway, I was thinking I should do something super cool. To get me out of the house, and have some fun."

My dad took the bait without hesitation. "That sounds like a great idea. What did you have in mind?"

"Well, I have always wanted to go skydiving."

He tilted his head, and frowned. "I don't know, Leese. That's dangerous."

"Actually, it's not!" I countered. "There's only a .0007 percent chance of an accident, plus I'd be with a trained instructor. It's no more dangerous than biking." I'd made the last part up on the spot (oops!) but the rest of it I'd read on the internet (which means it must be true.)

"Hmm." My dad titled his head and shrugged as if he was both astonished and assured. "Sounds fun! Good luck convincing your mother."

"Please help me!" I whined.

He rubbed his hand over his chin, which was something that he did when he was thinking. After a long silence, he finally agreed. "Alright, I'll see what I can do."

"Yay! Thank you Daddy!" I jumped up and down for dramatic effect. Then I ran over and gave him a hug. After all that talking and moving and acting I was worn out, so I dragged myself back up to my room and laid down.

I have no clue how my dad did it. All I know is that when I woke up the next morning my mom was in agreement, however tentatively. It was settled, I would go skydiving! I called Jesse immediately, before

THE BUCKET LIST

I fully realized what I was doing.

"Hey!" he exclaimed in an exuberant voice.

"Hi. So, I convinced my parents. Any luck with yours?"

He paused. "That's great... unfortunately, mine are not so easily persuaded. I'm still working on it, you know, laying on the guilt. My mom's starting to come around, she'll be more likely to say yes once I tell her your parents have agreed."

"Okay. Just let me know."

"Of course, Leesie."

I smiled. "Alright, well... see you I guess."

"Bye," he replied.

"Xtreme Thrillz: Skydiving and Fun," Jesse read out loud, squinting at the building complex in front of us. I felt the nervous excitement accumulating in my gut.

I took a deep breath. "Ready?"

"As I'll ever be," Jesse answered.

After a long lecture on safety and proper skydiving procedures and whatnot, we were finally ready to head up into the clouds.

Two instructors and a pilot led us to a car, which drove us to a reserved spot at the local airport. The instructor who was driving was grinning away the whole time, obviously excited to spread his love of skydiving to a few newbies. He showed us the plane and opened the metallic door, waving his hand, gesturing for us to follow him inside. "Don't be shy!"

Because it was our first time, Jesse and I both had to be "supervised" as they called it, which meant we had to be attached to someone else. The instructor I was with, Oscar or Tony or something, was simply ecstatic about the jump; he clearly loved skydiving. His enthusiasm was contagious, but somehow it managed to multiply my anxiety.

Jesse jumped first. He offered to let me go before him, but I chickened out. After he jumped, I stood in the doorway, watching him get smaller and smaller, and I started to panic. I was crazy. Why would I ever dream of doing something as idiotic as jumping out of a plane?

Oscar or Tony or whatever told me that I couldn't wait much longer, because we had to land in the right spot or something. Finally, he counted down from three and we jumped.

It wasn't as scary as I thought it would be. Despite being assured otherwise by the training video, I had expected it to feel like I was falling off of a cliff. Instead I was soaring, not plunging to my imminent death. And for the first time in a long time, I felt free. I felt happy.

When I talked to Jesse after landing, he was still super psyched up from the adrenaline. I was too, of course, but his showed quite a bit more. He practically screamed, "That was awesome! Holy mother of God that was-"

"Jesse! Shh," I scolded him before he could permanently damage my eardrums.

"You're such a buzzkill," he whispered so softly I could barely make out what he was saying.

He didn't seem buzz-killed however; he transitioned right back into hyper-Jesse in a few moments. And he stayed that way the whole time we were getting ready to leave.

"That was crazy, wasn't it?!" Jesse kept shouting, until we got to the car.

"Yup..." I agreed half-heartedly. "You want me to drive? You seem a bit high-strung."

"Nah."

"Okay..."

Of course, Jesse drove like a maniac on the way back. And he wouldn't shut up. "It was the best! Wasn't it? Don't tell me you didn't love it, Leese!"

☑ Go skydiving

☐ PLAY HIDE AND SEEK IN IKEA

That night, amid my tossing and turning, I came to accept the fact that finishing Tate's bucket list was an obligation, and I decided it could even be something I'd enjoy.

I eventually gave up on sleeping; sometimes an idea infects your mind and makes it impossible to rest. So I lay awake in bed, trying to figure out the best way to complete the next few items on the list. The next goal was to play hide and seek in an Ikea. After mulling it over for quite awhile, I decided it was time to initiate a plan.

Me: *Hey guys, I'm going to play hide and seek at Ikea tomorrow, anyone want to come? Text back and I'll give you the details.*

I pressed send, and started waiting for a response. Then I realized that it was four AM. No one was going to be awake. Oh well, they'd get it in the morning. So I rested my head once more on my pillow, closing my eyes and finally falling into an agitated sleep.

Tate and I drove up to the dimly lit carnival. The circus colors, the bell-toned fanfare, and the joyful people were all there, but the atmosphere was bleak, dark. "What do you think is going on here?" I asked Tate. She didn't say anything, but laughed and tossed her head to get the cashew-blonde hair out of her face.

We got out of the car and peered around. The whole world looked as if it were a sepia photograph in live action. I couldn't make out the faces of anyone except for Tate; hers was as clear as daylight.

Tate suddenly grabbed my hand and led me over to the ferris wheel. There wasn't anybody on the wheel, so we clambered into one of the empty chairs. Almost instantly, Tate climbed right back out. "What are you doing?" I questioned irritably. "We haven't ridden the ride yet."

She looked at me, confused. "The ride's long ridden, Leese," Tate said in a voice that sounded just slightly different than usual.

Then she walked over to a giant mirror maze. I followed. There was a man, presumably a carnie, sitting on a stool right outside the maze, who I swore I recognized. For whatever reason, Tate and the man looked at each other and began sharing a foreign laughter. Then, Tate took off into the maze.

I watched her disappear around the corner, and I ran to follow, my reflections in the shoulder-high mirrors blurring as I sped past. "Tate!" I called as I turned the corner.

I was barely able to catch a glimpse of her before she turned and vanished around another corner, laughing as though it was all a game.

I felt a panic growing in my gut as I followed her. Why wasn't she waiting for me? While I was running, the mirrors grew taller, so that before long I couldn't see over them. This made it impossible to keep an eye on Tate, and every time she disappeared from my sight I felt my franticness expand a bit. I had to resort to following the sound of her gleeful laughter. But as we kept running, and the mirrors grew taller still, the laughter became silence.

"Tate!" I kept shouting, alternatively with gasping for air. I didn't stop running though. I had to catch her. I had to. If I didn't, something unspeakably bad was going to happen. I wasn't sure what, but I knew it would be something horrendous.

The mirrors were growing ever taller, while Tate was to growing less and less cheerful. She started looking back at me whenever we were in sight of each other with a worried, almost suspicious expression.

"Tate," I gasped when it felt like my lungs were punctured, "Tate, wait up."

"Stop following me!" she responded defensively, almost as though she didn't know who I was, then continued running away.

I kept chasing her, as the mirrors were becoming colossal in size, and my reflections got more and more distorted. I knew I had to catch up, but Tate was always a turn ahead of me. I could always just barely see which way she went next.

Tate started crying, a panicked, desperate cry. It sounded the way I felt. But she kept running. "Stop following me!" she screamed hysterically.

I slowed to a stop. Was she really talking to me? Was I the reason she was crying? Tate kept running, and in a horrible moment I realized that I could never catch her. She would always run just a bit farther, just a bit faster, or just a bit longer.

I collapsed onto my knees as tears began streaming down my face. I felt an angry, panicked sort of sadness. I felt like there was nothing I could do, but that I had to do something.

I turned to the side and felt my heart shudder in fear. Someone was staring at me from the circus mirror on the side of the maze. A girl, one I had never seen before. I reached out. She reached out. I tilted my head. She tilted her head.

I kept extending my arm toward the mirror, and the strange girl kept extending hers. Finally, when our skin touched, the whole maze began exploding. The sound of thousands of glass mirrors shattering at once echoed throughout the desolate wasteland I was left standing in. The earth was falling apart around me; mirrors were collapsing, the strange girl was peering into my eyes, and Tate was still running further and further away from me.

I spun around, as the shadow of a monumental rectangular mirror loomed over my terrified, traumatized, tiny self. I tried to run, but the mirror still fell. I couldn't outrun it, and the terrible, deafening noise still rumbled. And then, it hit me.

Naturally, I woke up at that point, to find that the noise was real.

However, the sound had not come from an avalanche of mirrors, but from my phone. It was vibrating almost nonstop.

I took it off of the bedside table, pressing the lock button. Twenty-three new messages. Well alrighty then. I guess my friends really wanted to go to Ikea and play some hide and seek.

No, of course it wasn't that. The best friend of the girl who'd killed herself had made contact with the outside world for the first time in weeks. This was a serious occasion; I expected the local news station to show up quite soon to capture my interview.

I scrolled painstakingly through the texts. Ella answered straightforwardly, *Sure*. However, nearly everyone else's responses could've been pulled right out of a Shakespearean drama. Jesse was the only one who hadn't responded.

I sent a text saying that we'd meet at Ikea at three, and then tried to drown out my phone's endless buzzing due to the excessive amount of responses. After a few minutes of non-stop notifications, I finally decided I needed to leave my room to get some time away from my phone.

I made my way downstairs in search of breakfast, which was something I hadn't done in ages. When I sauntered into the kitchen, both of my parents gaped, then took a few moments to shake off the surprise. I smiled as they both started talking at once about how I was up so early and offered me toast. It felt so familiar: my dad sitting at the table with a newspaper sprawled about and a mug of coffee in his hand, and my mom leaning against the counter with a glass of orange juice. Those things were things I knew, things that felt natural and right.

After a few minutes of casual conversation, I asked my mom, "Can I use the car today?"

"Sure," she agreed easily. "Where are you going?"

"Umm..." I tried to decide how to say it without sounding weird, but I couldn't, so I simply answered, "Ikea."

My dad grinned. He was positively radiant. I have no idea why. "Oh, I love Ikea!"

Frankly, my parents were insanely lucky that they got such an honest kid. I could have easily tricked them, and they'd never know. I wouldn't dream of doing that, of course, which is why they were extremely blessed.

As my car rumbled across the grimy pavement of the Ikea parking lot, I glanced around. None of my friends had shown up yet, and I didn't have a single inkling about how many would. I was a few minutes early; I'd told everyone to wait outside the front of the store on the benches, and no one was there yet. I waited on the cement patio, in a state of anxiety and anticipation.

Before I knew it, the crowd I had invited was standing before me, along with a few people I hadn't. The first to arrive was Ella, who greeted me with a, "Hey," and immediately shot into conversation. It was nice and not awkward. More and more people arrived, and every one of them reacted to me a bit differently than the one before. Some tried to act normal, but I could tell they were holding something back. Others went in for a passionate warm hug, which I hesitantly had to accept.

Once almost everyone was there, and the tension had died down a little, a minivan pulled up. Jesse opened the passenger's door while his mom nagged him about something.

"Yes, yes I know! Mom, I gotta go!" He shut the door while she was still talking, turned around, and flashed a smile at the group. Then he strolled up to us, hands shoved deep within his pockets.

Suddenly, it occurred to me that no one else there officially knew Jesse. Sure, they had probably heard of him and seen him around school, but they'd probably never been formally introduced. "Oh, guys, this-" I began.

"Jesse, nice to meet you all," he cut me off. Then he went around to every single member of the group, shaking hands. He reached me last, took my hand in his, and whispered, "I think they like me." At first, I thought he was joking, so I laughed. But, it won me a weird look from him, which made me think he was actually serious.

I tried to pave over the awkwardness by briefly going over the rules. We assigned Jake as the first seeker, and the cue was given for everybody else to sprint inside and get to hiding. Some of us tried to blend in, while some hid under beds and behind couches.

A few minutes in, I decided to change spots. I peered around quickly, making sure that no one I knew was nearby. However, even though I was positive that I'd checked thoroughly, I didn't make it ten paces from my hiding spot before I noticed Jake searching close by. I frantically ducked behind a rug that was on display, and held my breath, praying that he hadn't seen me. Luckily, when I peeked my head out a few seconds later, he was gone.

"Ma'am, can I help you?" the voice of an old woman came from next to me. I turned quickly to see an employee with white hair and a menacing expression staring at me.

"No, I, uh, just wanted to see the back of this rug," I blurted hastily. Her face was painted with disbelief. "It's very nice," I added, stroking it as if it were a puppy.

"Alright..." She nodded and walked away, but I spotted her whispering to another employee and staring at me a minute later.

Miraculously, I managed to get third place the first round. The second didn't go nearly as well: I was found first, which meant I had to seek next.

As I stood up after checking under a bed, the cranky white-haired lady was on my back again. "Ma'am, please do not to get on the floor. If you don't stop making the other customers uncomfortable, we're going to have to request that you to leave." I didn't answer. I merely gave a half nod in response. Maybe I should've stopped then, but I kept going. I wasn't about to let some random old lady get to me.

By the sixth round, most of my friends had left. Apparently they'd been talked to by the employees as well. Only Jesse, Ella, and I were left playing; we had no intentions of quitting yet.

It was even more fun with just the three of us. Jesse was the seeker, while Ella and I did the thing where we ran to the spot he'd just checked once he moved on. We were laughing wildly, and Jesse was practically chasing us, when what do you know, the White Menace appeared in front of us.

"You three are going to have to leave. I'm sorry that you're not mature enough to be in a furniture store."

"Take it easy, we're just playing a friendly game of hide and seek. Found you, by the way." Jesse tapped both of our shoulders.

"Get out of this store or I'm calling the manager," she scolded sternly. We silently decided it would be a good idea to leave.

As we walked out, the lady called out to us, "Don't come back here again!"

I finished her sentence in a whisper, "you rotten kids!" We burst out laughing, but quietly, so she wouldn't know.

Jesse turned around after his fit of laughter, giving the lady an over enthusiastic thumbs up. Her expression was priceless.

"That was really fun!" Ella enthused after we'd finished with our fits of laughter. "How'd you come up with the idea?"

"Oh, you know... Pinterest," I lied. Jesse glanced over at me, slightly surprised. I looked away and started skimming the parking lot for my car, hoping the subject would drop.

I gave Jesse a ride back. I don't know why, but it happened. We lived a block away from each other, so it only made sense, I suppose. However, I was not mentally prepared for ten minutes of either dead silence or awkward conversation with him. "You didn't tell Ella about the bucket list," he remarked after we'd driven a few miles in utter silence. "You didn't seem afraid to tell me."

"Jesse, I didn't tell you. You happened across it while nosing through my room." He put his hands up in resignation to his guiltiness, and I chuckled. "No offense."

A brief but piercing awkward silence followed. Finally, Jesse inquired, "So what's next? On the list?"

"Oh, um, well..." No duh, we both knew what was next. Him asking that was more of a formality. In case you, dear reader, fail to recall, the next item on the bucket list was to go on a date with Jesse. I mumbled incoherently under my breath.

"Oh yes," he avowed with an understanding nod, "I do remember Tate always wanting to-" here he too mumbled incoherently in a rather mocking matter. "I seem to remember, and correct me if I'm wrong, that the next item on this list is actually going on a date with me."

"It would seem it is," I admitted grimly. It was silent after that, but I could practically hear the grin growing on Jesse's face loud and clear.

"Seven o'clock, this Friday. Dress fancy." I had nothing else to do but roll my eyes and groan in approval. By that point, we'd arrived at his house, and he gave me a self-assured look before getting out of the car.

☑ Play hide and seek in Ikea

☐ GO ON A DATE WITH JESSE

I stomped upstairs to my room, where I let my phone fall from my hands and clatter onto the bedside table. I felt exhausted; it had been a while since I'd been so active and social. After grabbing one of Tate's old books, I let my body go limp across my bedspread.

I caught a glimpse of the bucket list, and stared at it for a minute. "I bet you feel real smug about yourself right now," I fumed. It had reason to be, because I was now going on a date with the *last* person I'd ever want to go on a date with. I cracked open the story, and let my thoughts about the date drift away.

As I was reading, something fell out of the pages from the near-end of the book. I bent over and found myself face-to-face with Tate's school picture from awhile back. Eighth grade, maybe.

After a moment, I gently picked up the picture. It was so weird to think that the girl staring up at me, with the wide braced smile, was dead. It was weird to think that that Tate was the same Tate that didn't bother saying goodbye. I couldn't believe that the Tate in the picture was the same girl who was in the coffin at the funeral.

As I mentioned earlier, the funeral was probably the worst five hours I have ever experienced. It was when things really sunk in.

I had to eulogize. I mean, nobody made me, but how could I say no when my late best friend's parents asked me to I speak at her funeral? So I talked about Tate. I told the story of when we first met. I talked about how she was funny, and adventurous, and confident. I didn't mention that, in her last months, Tate lost all of these characteristics.

I didn't once say anything about high school. The only stories I told were from middle or elementary school. I didn't talk about the last time I had seen Tate. I pretended she'd remained the old her: happy, creative, and mine. It made a better story that way.

As I was speaking, my eyes found Jesse's in the crowd. I wondered if he knew I was bending the truth. I wondered if he too would've had to lie or disappoint if he were eulogizing.

"Tate Jordyn Conscivit. She was my advisor, my confidant, my childhood playmate. But most importantly, Tate was my best friend." I tried not to cry as I spoke, and I think I was surprisingly successful, considering the circumstances.

"I met Tate when we were eight years old. And almost instantly, we became closer than sisters." I didn't know if that part was true, because neither she nor I had a sister, so I had no comparison. It sounded sweet, though.

I talked some more about playing together as kids, but I couldn't get through everything I'd written. I could hear Tate's mom crying and there was an excruciatingly painful lump in my throat that wouldn't go away.

Thankfully, the funeral wasn't open coffin. Nobody said so, but everyone knew that her body wouldn't look quite right. Her neck was probably all black and blue. I don't think I could've survived if I had seen her, lying there, cold as stone. I had barely survived as it was.

I tried to avoid reliving that day as much as possible, but it still managed to creep into my mind nearly everyday.

Shaking my head, I brought myself back to reality. I gave up on reading, shut the book, returned it to my bookshelf, and tucked the picture under one of the ribbons on my bulletin board.

I turned on my instrumental music channel on Pandora, then plopped down on my bed and fell into a trance. For an hour or so, I cycled through critical thought and complete mindlessness.

Around six, I heard my mom shouting that dinner was ready. I didn't go downstairs though, and I don't think she was expecting me to. I hadn't been attending meals much. Half an hour later she brought up some chicken, which was awesome, because I was starving.

"Whatcha up to?" she queried.

I shrugged. "Nothing really."

"Alright. Well, your father and I were going to play some Scrabble if you'd like to join us."

"No, thanks," I responded.

"Okay. If you change your mind, we'll be downstairs."

She left and shut the door softly behind her. I turned back to my room, suddenly restless, but unsure of what to do with myself. Absentmindedly, I strolled over to my desk, where the bucket list lay innocently. I picked it up and scanned it.

Jesse and I had both remembered wrong. The next item was, in fact, not going on a date with him, but rather to watch all of the *Twilight* movies in one day. After some contemplation, I decided I was more fearful of the movies than the date.

However, I couldn't do either of those things that night. After carefully reading over the list several times, I decided to begin conquering number twenty-one: working at Hollister. I pulled out my computer and searched for the Hollister website.

You cannot even imagine my pleasure when I discovered that the Hollister at the mall nearby was accepting applications. You can't imagine it because it didn't exist. Working at Hollister sounded about as fun as taking the ACT. Twice.

Nevertheless, I printed an application and filled it out in my finest handwriting. I didn't know who to use as references, but by that point, it was nearly eight, and I was getting lazy (again). So I figured I'd ask my dad for help the next day.

As I was laying in bed that night, I realized that when I woke up it would be Thursday. This thought made me audibly groan, because after Thursday often comes Friday. And Friday was the day of the date. Ugh...

I didn't want to be, but was, worried about what I was going to wear. I mean, he said dress nice, but I didn't know where we were going. How fancy was I supposed to dress? Clearly, Jesse didn't understand that there are many varying degrees of formal attire.

This is stupid, I told myself. *You don't even like him.* And I didn't. But I still wanted to look pretty. I tried not to think about it by rolling over and focusing every ounce of my attention on falling asleep, which is an awful way to fall asleep. Nevertheless, within half an hour, I was out cold.

*Jesse took a deep breath as he stared at his reflection in the mirror. Today was the day. He decided he looked good enough, then went into the kitchen where his mom was waiting to drive him and his little brother, Graham, to Batavia Lake Middle School.

When Jesse walked into English class, he saw Leesie already sitting at her desk. But she was talking to Tate and two other girls. He couldn't approach her with others around; that'd be too awkward.

Then at lunch, Leesie was with tons of classmates once again. Jesse was getting increasingly anxious. If he didn't ask her today, he might lose his nerve. Fortunately, right before school ended, he saw her standing alone getting books out of her locker. It was his chance.

He forced himself to walk up to her and flash what he thought was a charming smile. It probably looked more like a grimace. "Hi, Leesie."

"Oh, hey Jesse," she greeted brightly. Her smile was so... captivating.

"I've been wondering... you know, if you don't already... well, you see..."

She tilted her head, causing her dirty-blond hair to swish, and looked at him confusedly. Ahh, he was messing this up, wasn't he? He should spit it out already. "Do you want to go to the Spring Formal with me?"

Leesie's face fell. That couldn't be a good sign. "I'm so sorry. I...

uh, I can't. I'm not allowed."

"Oh," Jesse said, trying not to look too crestfallen. He knew she was lying, of course, but that wasn't what was bothering him. What he really nagging at him was the fact that Leesie didn't want to go with him, when he had been almost positive she liked him. Like, like liked him. "That's okay."

"Sorry." She looked rather miserable, which somehow seemed to embellish her already impressive prettiness. "I have to go."

"Bye."

"Bye." And with that, she left, and Jesse saw her catch up to Tate in the crowd. The two of them walked side-by-side toward the bus, probably talking about what a doofus he was.

And right before they disappeared from view, Tate turned her head and stared straight at him, with something that looked suspiciously like longing in her discouraged blue eyes.

The following day, I was dragged out of the safe walls of my room at eight in the morning. "We've got another talk session, remember?" my mom said with a gleeful smile. Ugh. I remembered her briefly mentioning therapy, but I also remember me briefly refusing. Apparently, she'd hoped I had forgotten about my denial.

Jenni was once again ecstatic to see us. My mom waited in the lobby; I suppose she'd decided I was okay on my own. Which was good, considering that (technically, legally) I was an adult.

"So what's new with you, Leesie?" she questioned, as though we were old friends catching up.

"Well, I've been working on some of the things on the list," I responded dully.

Her face lit up like a Christmas tree. "That's great!"

"Yeah." I nodded, though I didn't see the greatness factor.

"What've you done so far?" She leaned forward in her seat, apparently extraordinarily interested.

I thought for a moment, choosing how to answer. "Skydiving."

She was rather surprised at my blunt response, naturally. But, after a moment, she recovered. "Oh, great! Did you enjoy it?" Her tone made it sound as if she was my buddy, not my therapist.

"Yeah," I answered in a monotone. I didn't feel up for humoring her for the sake of humoring her. However, the following silence was slightly uncomfortable.

"Cool. Uh, so have you done anything else?" she pressed, trying to get me to open up.

"Yeah," I repeated. Jenni nodded.

I realized that if I kept dead ending her, things would become even more awkward.

"Well, also, I went and played hide and seek at an Ikea. There was this crazy old lady who I named 'the White Menace.'"

Jenni laughed. The rest of the session went marginally better.

On Friday, I considered inviting Ella over to help me get ready, but I figured she would be curious as to why I was going on a date with Jesse. I didn't want to tell her about the bucket list, but I also didn't want her to think I was going of my own free will. All in all, I ended up getting ready alone. But let's face it, Ella wasn't who I wanted anyway.

Yet, Tate had left me, so I was alone. We'd always imagined that someday I'd help her get ready for a date with Jesse. Now I was helping myself.

I didn't spend the whole day prepping for the date. But, to be honest, I had nothing else to do, so I pretty much spent the whole day prepping for the date.

First I painted my nails, a pale turquoise that matched the necklace I'd be wearing. Then I got dressed and did my hair. Finally, I moved on to my makeup. After way more preparation than was realistically needed, I decided I was presentable.

I was done getting ready by 6:30, so I ended up switching off between browsing Tumblr and nervously pacing around my room.

When seven o'clock arrived, so did Jesse. He was not a second late, nor a second early. His promptness was frightening.

Not only was he on time, he was dressed to the nines, wearing a suit. I felt slightly informal in my plain black dress. Holding out a dozen red roses, he greeted me, "Evening, Elise." I smiled, not bothering to get angry over him using my full name. "You look gorgeous. Absolutely stunning!"

I almost laughed. "Thanks. You're not too bad yourself."

He shrugged. "I wanted to be as Tate-worthy as possible." I felt sadness gripping at my gut. Jesse noticed the change, and tried to distract me from it. "Shall we?" He gestured back to the driveway where his car was parked.

"Of course." I set the roses onto the small table next to the door and followed him outside.

He opened the car door for me. He repeated this in the same mannerly fashion once we'd reached the restaurant. Then he opened the restaurant door for me. Once we were shown our table, he pulled out my chair. It was all very romantic. Tate would've loved it.

"The chivalry just doesn't end with you, does it?" I remarked, after Jesse waited for me to be seated before himself.

"Nah, it's no chivalry. A gentleman knows to be mannerful and impressive when there's someone worth being mannerful and impressive for." I'll admit, I may have blushed a little at that. "Of course, I'm only saying that because we've got to make this date genuine, otherwise it doesn't count." He grinned, and I rolled my eyes.

La Salle Élégante was a restaurant that you would only go to on a date, or for your great aunt's birthday. It was fancy and quiet, with classical music playing softly in the background. A formally dressed, cute waiter appeared and asked us what we wanted to drink.

I almost got water, but then thought, W*hat would Tate get?* So, I ended up ordering the fanciest sounding non-alcoholic drink on the menu. "I'll have a virgin peach daiquiri punch."

Jesse raised his eyebrows questioningly but ended up ordering the same thing.

"So, Leesie, how are you?" Jesse inquired, staring at me intently.

Feeling somewhat uncomfortable under his intense gaze, I awkwardly nodded and answered, "Good." After a moment of quiet, I added, "And you?"

Jesse took his time in thinking. "Well, as good as can be expected, I suppose. Been playing a lot of lacrosse."

I nodded. Jesse had played lacrosse during all four of our years in high school. He was actually pretty decent.

When I didn't say anything, he continued, "How about you? What've you been up to?"

I honestly had no clue how to answer that question. What had I been doing lately? "Not too much."

"Come on, summing up your whole life since I last saw you with, 'not too much'? Leesie. What've you been up to?"

"Well, I applied for a job at Hollister," I relented. "It's on the bucket list, you know."

"That's awesome! Are you excited to work there?"

I gave him a look. A please-don't-make-me-answer-that look.

He nodded, hearing what was not said. "On the bright side, money."

I laughed. "Yeah. That I am looking forward to."

"What are you going to spend it on?"

I thought for a moment. "I was thinking of buying some depressing music on iTunes, to drown out my sorrows."

Jesse wasn't quite sure how to react to that. Finally, he contended with, "But we need that money for some of the more expensive things on the bucket list."

Eventually, we both ended up leaning over my phone, studying a picture of the bucket list and talking about the logistics of completing it before summer was over.

"I don't think it's possible," I told him with a frown.

"We can do it. There are twenty-nine things on the list, and you've already done four of them. Five once this fine evening comes to a conclusion. And don't forget that half of it is nice and easy. Dancing under the stars, for example."

"Yeah," I retorted, "but some are much harder. Like, going to the top of the Eiffel Tower, or standing under the Hollywood sign."

"It'll be fine," he persisted. "We get jobs as soon as possible to get money for the traveling, and meanwhile we'll work on the easy parts of the list."

"Okay," I agreed.

"We got this, Leese," he grinned and I reluctantly smiled back. We were a team.

When we pulled back into my driveway, Jesse opened the car door for me yet again. It was nearly ten. The sun had reluctantly gone to bed, and the dark night surrounded us, bringing with it a certain peace that simply could never be found in daylight. Jesse peered up at the twinkling stars, and I followed his gaze.

"How about we knock one more thing off of the list, while we have the opportunity?" Jesse suggested, causing me to tear my eyes away from the sky. I saw he was holding his hand out to me. "May I have this dance?"

"You may," I answered softly. I took Jesse's hand and let him pull me in. He put his arms around me, and I copied the action.

It was perfect; the air was warm, but not humid like it was during the day, and the nearly absolute silence made it feel as though no one existed except Jesse and me.

I'm not sure exactly how long we were standing there, swaying to a nonexistent beat, but I think it was a long time. And yet it felt to be no time at all. Sadly, even no time had an end, and too soon the song that had never been playing was over.

Jesse let go of my waist, causing me to awaken from a trance I hadn't realized I'd been in. "Check," he beamed, drawing an imaginary check mark in the air. One more thing was crossed off the bucket list. I blushed and broke into a smile. He grinned back, then peered at his watch.

"We should probably part ways. Get to bed, maybe," he advised, and I nodded in agreement. "But hey, you tell me when you're ready to tackle another goal on that list, Leesie. It's *our* thing now."

I hesitated a minute before responding as casually as I could, "Sure." He flashed me one last grin for the evening, then turned and walked towards his car.

"Night, Jesse."

- [x] Go on a date with Jesse
- [x] Dance under the stars

☐ WATCH ALL THE TWILIGHT MOVIES IN ONE DAY

Some girls love the feeling of spending hours and hours preparing themselves for a perfect night: doing their hair, nails, makeup, blah blah blah. Me? I love taking everything off in the span of five minutes and feeling a rush of comfort as I hop into bed. It's not that I hated getting ready, but it felt so much better to get un-ready.

But even with the glorious comfort that comes from changing into sweatpants, I was restless that night. I tossed and turned, trying not to over-analyze, but, you know, at night... thoughts are thought. At first, I was innocently reliving some of the moments of the night: the highlights, the awkward parts, the dancing. It wasn't bad in any way, until a thought crept into my mind. *This night should have been Tate's.*

Like a kick to the stomach, it took my breath away. I didn't have enough self-control to stop myself from going further. I wondered what Tate would've worn, how she would've responded to certain questions, and what she would've been feeling. Needless to say, I didn't sleep much that night.

Now, I realize that it seems like I spent seventy-five percent of my life sleeping and despite that I still suffered relentless exhaustion. That was not the case. While I did, in fact, suffer relentless exhaustion, and did, in fact, spend most of my hours in bed, I didn't spend a very large percentage of those hours sleeping. They were usually spent thinking, and tossing, and turning, and crying, with a bit of sleeping on the side. That night was more of the same.

I managed to sleep for a couple of hours in the morning though, and woke up in a good mood (at least compared to my usual mood.) I went downstairs, drank some orange juice, and by the time I went back up to my room, Jesse had texted me.

Jess: *what's next?*
Me: *Twilight marathon :/ Tonight?*
Jess: *Sure I'll bring the movies.*
Me: *You have them? :D*
Jess: *I know someone who knows someone*
Me: *Right... Be here at seven?*
Jess: *Okay. See ya then.*
Me: *Bye*

Precisely as he had done with the date, Jesse arrived eerily on time for the movie marathon. Opening the front door, I saw him holding blankets, pillows, soda, candy, and the movies.

"Wow."

"First thing you should know about me Leesie, but apparently don't: I always come prepared."

"Trust me Jess, I know." I sidestepped out of his way. He waddled into the living room and dropped the blankets and pillows onto the couch.

My mom ambled in from the kitchen and beamed. "Oh, hey Jesse."

"Hi, Mrs. Derell."

"Ahh, I wish we had more snacks for you two to munch on during your movies... Why don't you order some pizza?" my mom suggested. I took that to mean, "I will buy you pizza."

"That sounds yummy." I smiled, and after a minute, she left the room.

"Your mother is awesome!" Jesse whispered, causing me to crack up. "I've got Domino's on speed dial. Number one." I burst out laughing even harder, and nearly fell to the floor with delight when it proved true.

"Hi, Jeremy," Jesse said into the phone. "One sec." He put his hand against the microphone and asked me, "Pepperoni, I presume?"

I recovered from my laughing fit, and nodded. "Yeah!"

"Excellent." Then, directing his voice back into the phone, "We'll take a large pepperoni with some parm bites and you know I always need my Cinna Stix."

While we waited for the pizza guy, we set up for our movie-watching extravaganza. By the time he arrived, the previews were flashing on the screen.

We sat on the floor eating pizza through most of the decent, albeit cheesy, first movie.

The second movie was a bit more exciting because Taylor Lautner took his shirt off, but even those abs couldn't keep me entertained for the whole movie. Halfway through, I turned to Jesse and whined, "I'm so bored..."

He stared at me for a second wide-eyed, then grabbed my hand in both of his and whispered urgently, "Shh... it's getting good."

By the time the second movie was over, I knew I had made a major mistake. "I don't think finishing everything on the bucket list is all that important. Let's skip this one."

"Leesie Leese McLeesanator. No, no, no," he spewed. "All you need is to take a break. And I have a surprise for you. I brought you flours."

"Um..." I hesitated, slightly creeped out. "Okay."

Jesse reached over into his pile and pulled out two bags of baking flour. My thoughts jumped to "Bake in the middle of the night," which was on the bucket list.

I began shaking my head, letting it fall into my hands with fake disapproval.

"Come on, let's get baking."

It was about 11:30, which I suppose technically qualifies as the middle of the night. My parents were both asleep, it was pitch black out, and the house was dead silent, so the feeling was definitely there.

"What should we make?" I whispered.

"How much chocolate do you have in the house?"

I narrowed my eyes. "Why?"

Jesse answered quietly, "I was thinking we could make chocolate cake."

I grinned. I had never been crazier about an idea. And so we began.

I pulled out my mom's Betty Crocker cookbook. It was covered with stains and crumbs and spills; she used it for nearly everything she made in the kitchen. But I had to admit, the chocolate cake recipe in that book was to die for.

"Recipes are for the weak!" Jesse stage-whispered in a dramatic movie voice.

"Not using recipes with no baking experience is for the people who don't want good cake," I retaliated.

Jesse considered this for a moment, then cocked his head. "Fair point. We use the recipe, just this once."

We bustled around the kitchen, throwing eggs into bowls and melting butter in the microwave. I was definitely head chef, and Jesse did whatever I ordered him to do.

While he measured out a teaspoon of salt, I measured the milk in a liquid measuring cup and gleefully poured it into the bowl, causing a few minor splashes in the process.

I grabbed the mixer and turned it on, but accidentally pushed the button a bit too far. The whisks started turning at supersonic speed, and chocolatey goo flung out of the bowl and into every nook and cranny of the kitchen, but mostly onto Jesse.

By the time I managed (but let's be honest, I didn't try too hard) to turn it off, Jesse was thoroughly covered. His initial expression upon being bombarded with batter resembled a look of horror. This was proceeded by him grabbing a handful of flour from his bowl, and throwing it directly at me.

I screamed, laughed and grabbed a handful of flour myself. I threw it at him and it made his face a ghostly shade of white, and his hair become a sharp contrast from it's usual darkness. "You do not dare mess with The Jessmaster!"

An epic battle ensued. I will spare you the gory details. However, we had to stop shortly after the most intense part of the fight, due to an interference from the parental referee. We heard from upstairs, "Leesie, would you please shut up!" It was my dad, yelling from bed. After a fit of laughter, we managed to quiet down.

In the end, the cake was delicious, even though we messed up the measurements with our food fight. Somehow it worked out though, and the cake was so good we ate the entire thing while watching the fourth and fifth movies.

How do I put this? *Twilight* was, well... dull. In my humble opinion. Jesse's raptured attention from the beginning of the marathon faded extraordinarily by the end, and he was fast asleep during at least half of the last movie.

I, on the other hand, had a little more determination. I managed to sit through the last scenes of "Breaking Dawn - Part 2." Specifically, the final battle, which was incredibly boring. I was more or less gandering in the direction of the TV at that point, seeing but not watching. As soon as I saw the credits, I knew they were my cue to fall over and catch up on some much-needed sleep.

I woke up quite suddenly, thinking it was still the middle of the night. I quickly realized I was wrong when I saw light streaming in through the picture window. I was thinking about how pretty it was outside, when I saw movement out of the corner of my eye. I jolted, and looked over to see Jesse creepily staring at me from the living room desk.

After normalizing my heart rate, I sat up and said, "Hi..."

He let out an exasperated sigh and began, "I've been waiting nearly twenty minutes. I can't check it off for you, you know." He held out the bucket list.

I wasn't sure how I felt about that. On the one hand, I was excited to check one more thing off, but on the other, the fact that Jesse had the list meant he had been in my room. It's not that I don't trust him, but it's weird that he went in there without me knowing.

"Well, uh... thanks for going to the trouble of getting it, saves me the effort," I said hesitantly.

"Oh, and also, there's water coming out of your alarm," he stated, as if this were a serious issue.

I rolled my eyes, stood up, and grabbed the list. "It's supposed to do that."

After checking the little boxes next to "Watch all the *Twilight* movies in one day" and "Bake in the middle of the night," we agreed that pancakes were a thing that we needed. My dad was home, which meant an endless supply of pancakes at our demand.

"Dad?" I yelled. "Flapjacks."

"You got it, Leese!" I watched the jolly pancake-enthusiast that was my father coming down the stairs and walking into my kitchen. I couldn't see what he did next, but I knew from experience that he was putting on his white apron and would soon be getting out a mixing bowl with feverish passion.

"What the... what blew up in here!?" he suddenly yelled back, obviously seeing the remnants of our food fight. Jesse chuckled in remembrance, and I facepalmed as I recalled the gigantic mess we had to clean up.

☑ Watch all the Twilight movies in one day
☑ Bake in the middle of the night

☐ BUILD A TREEHOUSE

To my annoyance, I was awoken from a lengthy nap around seven that evening when my phone started ringing. Half awake, I grabbed it and groggily answered, "Hewwo?"

On the other line, a business-y sounding voice said, "Hello, this is Rita Louise, the manager at Hollister. Is this Elise Derell?"

"Oh, hi. Yes, I'm her," I stammered. "But, I go by Leesie."

"Hello, Leesie. I have reviewed your application, and I'm very interested in setting up an interview. Does tomorrow work for you?"

I checked my mental calendar; much like every other day that month, tomorrow was occupied only by moping around. "Yeah, tomorrow would be great. Any time."

"How about three?" Rita suggested.

I nodded, but after a moment I realized that she couldn't see me. "Three's good."

"Alright, see you then!"

"Thanks. See you tomorrow." As soon as she hung up, I plopped my head back onto the pillow and let out a groan. Waking up sucks.

Somehow, I managed to make myself presentable for the interview without having a panic attack. My mom tried to calm my nerves by hovering around and giving me tips. I think it helped. Or maybe her ever-presentness was what caused the anxiety. Either way,

I managed to make it to the mall without any meltdowns.

I pulled in to a parking spot and began my death march to the Hollister.

The mall by my house was the kind of place where I would run into someone from my school accidentally. I suppose, technically, that's what happened to me.

As he strutted out of Hollister in a button-down and tie, Jesse gave me a snarky, confident grin. I paused, but I was already nearly late for the interview, so I couldn't interrogate him about why he was applying for the job that I wanted.

Halfway through the interview, my chances were glimmering with hope. But they dramatically dulled when I was asked, "Why do you want to work here?"

If I were to give the honest answer, Rita would realize that I actually didn't enjoy Hollister, and only wanted to work there for money and sentimental reasons. So, I improvised. "I, uh, like the clothes."

"Really?" Oh no. She could sense the fear, like a predator in the wild.

I tried to smile. It probably came off as a grimace. "Yeah, you know... the, uh, yoga pants." Silence ensued.

Finally, she repeated, "You like the yoga pants here?"

"Yeah..."

Rita nodded slowly. "But couldn't you buy yoga pants someplace else? Almost every retail store has them."

"Yes, um," I stuttered. "See, the thing is, you guys have the, uh, you know, the best yoga pants. The good stuff."

Rita nodded and said decisively, "Okay." She moved on to ask me the next question from her list. I flushed so red, it probably looked like I was wearing clown make-up. "Will you be available consistently, or..." she spoke in a way that was basically screaming, "yeah yeah yeah, you're not getting the job," and it didn't exactly help with my nerves.

"Well, no. I will probably be leaving a lot." I had been trying to sound more casual, more relaxed. Big mistake. The second the words left my mouth, my blush reddened further. It was meant to be a joke. Who jokes in an interview?! People who are good with people, I'm not one of those people.

"Oh... um, okay." Rita chuckled a bit, but unsuradly.

"No, no," I tried to reassure her. "I'm free pretty much every day."

"That's great. I mean, this isn't your typical office job, you can take time off if you want."

"Well, I am hoping to go to France, if I can get enough money," I told her.

"Oh, that's great!" she replied excitedly. "It's beautiful there!"

I tried to smile as she continued down her list of questions. I also tried not to get my hopes up.

On my way home I decided to stop by Jesse's house, to do my interrogating in person. Let's just say I wasn't cheery. Jesse had decided to become my competition, which made getting the job ten times harder. I couldn't wrap my head around around the fact that he was trying to steal the job from right under my nose. What a jerk.

As he opened the door, he smiled and remarked, "Hey, Leesie!" His tone suggested that I was coming over for a picnic, not that I was seriously considering slapping him.

"What the heck, Jesse?" I interjected. I waited for his response, but was only answered with silence. I elaborated, "Why would you apply for the job? She's going to pick you over me now and I won't be able to finish the bucket list!"

"Whoa, Leese, calm down. I want to finish the bucket list too, and we can both work there. It's not like they only have one employee. Anyway, the bucket list was my idea in the first place."

I clenched my fists. "Yeah, but I found it, when you didn't even bother going to her house. And I was her best friend."

Jesse's face contorted. "The only reason you were ever Tate's best friend is because you stole her from me when we were eight."

"Oh, get over yourself," I almost shouted, then turned around and left. He didn't follow me. Frankly, I didn't want him to.

The day after my not exactly pleasant run-in with Jesse, I was slouched in a chair after church let out. The post-service coffee hour was by far the worst part of going to church. It was nothing but a bunch of overly nice people making small talk while drinking a vile brown liquid that made everybody who was already far too chatty even more lively.

After several minutes of ceaseless waiting, as I cracked my back on my uncomfortable, hard wooden chair, I noticed the church's bulletin board a few feet away. A thought occurred to me, and I decided to check it out.

Sure enough, there was a neon pink flyer posted to it, advertising "Mr. Perkin's Piano Lessons." After reading it, I tore off one of the dangling strips of paper with his email on it. I made a quick mental note to email him as soon as I got home, so "we can work out a situation that works for EVERYONE!"

I arrived home a couple hours later (or at least it felt like hours,) and emailed Perkins right away. There was nothing better to do.

I had never played piano, and I didn't have much interest in it. I was a ukulele girl. But, learning to play piano was on the bucket list. Plus, I might even like it.

After I sent an email to Mr. Perkins letting him know that I was interested, I was once again stuck in my pit of boredom and sadness. Despite my recent flurry of productivity, I was the same lonely and despairing girl when the business subsided. I suppose I had simply become better at hiding it from the world. And from myself.

So I spent the rest of that Sunday in bed, marathoning old episodes of *Psych* and grieving. Or, as my mom put it, feeling sorry for myself. I've heard it both ways.

The next morning, I was eating my fourth bowl of cereal, when I heard the doorbell ring. Naturally, I didn't want my puffs to become mush, so I brought my bowl with me to answer the door.

It was Jesse. It took me several moments to comprehend his appearance, because he was dressed rather unusually. He was wearing a hardhat and in his arms were several two-by-fours.

"Good morning, Leesie," he greeted me with a smile that's radiance would've blinded the sun. "I'm dropping by to see if you'd like to join me in building a treehouse. It's on the list, you know."

My anger towards him had not entirely faded, which led me to smirk and comment, "Do you really think you need a hard hat to build a treehouse?"

"Oh this?" Jesse pointed at his head, then remarked, "Nah, this was in case you were still mad at me. And, clearly, we've both forgiven each other, so I won't be needing it."

"Your assumptions may be the death of you someday," I warned, only half joking.

Jesse cocked his head and said in a sweet tone, "Leesie, darling, you know I trust you greatly, which is why I will take off this hat. Promise me my trust is not misplaced."

I rolled my eyes, then remembered my cereal. I took a large bite, swallowed, and chanted, "I promise."

Jesse set down the boards on the porch and took off his hard hat as I leaned on the doorframe and watched. "Now," he continued, "treehouse?"

"Sure, but let me bring this in." I turned and took my bowl to the sink and shouted to my mom, "I'm going to play outside."

We chose a tree in the woods behind my house, and began building. That first day, I hit my thumb with a hammer at least three times. But, as the week progressed, my aim improved bit by bit. By the third time Jesse had knocked on my door to go building, I had my thumb-injuries-per-day ratio down to one.

Jesse was surprisingly handy, and even though I wasn't, I was having a lot of fun building the treehouse. With his expertise and my enthusiasm, we managed to finish the treehouse after three days. As he was nailing in the last board, Jesse asked me, "So, what's next on the list?"

"Zip-line, party all night, and sleep under the stars, I think."

"Well, well, well... Correct me if I'm wrong, but I'd say we just built ourselves a sleeping under the stars platform."

I thought about it. "Huh, I suppose we did."

"It's settled then," he concluded. "Tonight, we shall sleep here in our sleeping bags. Meet me at nine, and bring snacks."

Before I had the chance to respond, Jesse climbed out of the tree and was briskly walking back toward his house. He was one for dramatic exits, that's for sure.

The problem with sleeping outside, at night, unchaperoned, with a teenage boy, is that it's not exactly the easiest thing to convince your parents to allow. I had to plan my sales pitch carefully to assure its success.

"So, Mom," I started, that afternoon, "you know how Jesse and I have been working so hard the last few days building that treehouse?"

The monotonous response was not what I was hoping for, but it was what I got, and frankly, what I expected. "Uh, huh?"

"Well, we were thinking, what good is a house if it doesn't shelter you, at least for a bit? So, we devised a plan. Tonight, with your blessing, we will have a campout there in our house, to guarantee its worthiness." After saying that, I suddenly realized how much like Jesse I sounded. Apparently, he had rubbed off on me.

"Hmm," my mother answered, in that way moms answer that evokes worry and stress deep in the soul of the teenage inquirer.

I stayed silent, and tried to smile in a cute little girl sort of way.

"I don't know, Leese. You've been spending an awful lot of time with that boy," my mom began.

"Mom, this isn't some random idea of ours. It's an obligation. It's fate. Do you want all of our hard work to be for nothing? Plus, this is Jesse we're talking about here. He's practically your own son."

She sighed. "I don't really see the logic in that... but I suppose. Go ahead." I gave her a quick hug in thanks, then pulled out my phone to tell Jesse the news.

Me: *Game on.*

Jess: *you better bring snacks. my appetite skyrockets at around ten and doesn't die til about two.*

Me: *Bring your own snacks*

Jess: *But your house has better snacks*

Me: *Fineee. Funyuns, oreos, or chex*

Jess: *All three*

That night, I stumbled down to the treehouse while carrying my sleeping bag, pillow, and lots and lots of snacks. It was a bit of a hike to get there, and by the time I reached the treehouse there were leaves, sticks, and dirt covering my sleeping bag. We won't even talk about my hair.

I saw Jesse already sitting up in the tree, drinking a mountain dew and reaching into a bag of doritos. "You brought your own snacks!" I exclaimed, accusingly, while struggling to climb the ladder of the treehouse.

"Yeah, and now we have twice the snacks," Jesse deduced. "Win-win."

I finally reached the top of the ladder and scrambled onto the wooden platform we'd worked so hard to build. "Chex me," he held out his hand, and I bitterly dumped everything I was carrying on top of him.

Once Jesse had escaped the mountain of food, he nearly yelled, "I remember myself saying Chex, not Chex, sleeping bag, pillow, another pillow, Oreos, Cheetos, fruit snacks, and what, like twelve bags of Funyuns?"

"You forgot this," I mentioned, showing him the miniature battery-powered iPod dock I'd brought.

"Ah, yes, and the purple speaker, I didn't say that either." He rummaged through the pile and grabbed the bag of Chex Mix. "It's okay, baby," he comforted it. "You're safe with me now."

We settled down, laid out our sleeping bags, and made ourselves comfy.

"See that right there?" Jesse pointed to an unusually bright star. "That's our neighbor, Venus. Actually the hottest planet in the-" he suddenly paused. "Oh wait, no, nevermind, that's not Venus." I laughed as the guy tried desperately to prove his knowledge of astronomy.

After he gave up on that, I turned on the dock and plugged in my MP3 player. "Why do you use a Shuffle?" Jesse inquired.

"There's freedom in not having to choose," I replied.

"Hmph," was his only response.

I thought about it for a moment, then added, "That sounded way deeper than I meant it to." He chuckled, and we both fell silent and gazed back up at the stars, as the first song began.

It was "Distance" by Christina Perri. Not too fitting, but it had a nice tune.

I'm not sure exactly when I fell asleep. But I did, and when I woke up, my whole body hurt as though I'd run a marathon. The sun was beginning to rise, painting the sky pink. I repeatedly shook Jesse until he opened his eyes. "Look," I instructed him.

He propped himself up on his elbows and beheld at the sunrise. "That's really nice, Leesie. But why must life hurt so badly?"

I grinned. "It may not be a great house, but it's a house." I rubbed a knot in my left shoulder.

Jesse yawned and reached for one of the many bags of Funyuns. "Breakfast time."

"Eww, Jess, Funyuns for breakfast?"

He shrugged. "Would you prefer if I had something else?"

"Uh, yeah."

He nodded, thinking. "Okay," he stated after a minute. "You want me to eat something more breakfast-y?"

I nodded hesitantly. Suspicion was creeping into my mind.

"Okay." Jesse grabbed the fruit snacks. "Fruit is both nutritious and breakfast-y, I don't know what more you could possibly want from me."

I rolled my eyes and didn't bother dignifying him with a response, then grabbed a pack for myself.

It was breakfast-y enough for us.

- ☑ Build a treehouse
- ☑ Sleep under the stars

☐ WORK AT HOLLISTER

By the time I managed to get all my stuff back to my house, I had trooped to and from the treehouse three times. When I finally plopped down onto my bed, I was exhausted.

So, I spent a few hours sitting there catching up on my Youtube subscriptions and checking social media. As I was scrolling down my Tumblr feed, my phone dinged. Checking it, I saw that I'd gotten an email from the piano guy.

Dear Leesie,
My apologies for the delayed response. I am so happy to hear you are interested in learning to play the wonderful instrument that is the piano. You said you are open almost any day, and I have checked my schedule. The optimum day for me would be Monday nights at six o'clock. Let me know how this suits you. Hope to see you soon!
Edward Perkins
 Piano Prodigy, Piano Passionare, Piano Professor

It was official: he was a wackjob. He seemed kind of nice, though. I responded that Mondays would be fine and began mentally preparing for what I would be enduring in only three days.
Later that night, while I was binging Vsauce videos, a number called me that my phone didn't recognize. "Hello?"
"Hi. Is this Elise Derell?"

"Yes..."

"Leesie, this is Rita."

"Oh, hello," I remarked dumbly, not recognizing the name.

"I'm calling to tell you that we'd like to offer you a position here at Hollister."

I was shocked. When I finally recomposed myself, I sputtered, "Oh, great! That's great!" I wondered how many people applied. Maybe it was only Jesse and I. "I would definitely like to accept the offer."

"Can you be here on Monday from nine to three?"

"Yeah," I assured her.

"Alright, see you then."

"Thank you. Bye."

I put down the phone dumbfoundedly. Well, that happened. Maybe I didn't do as badly as I'd thought in the interview. Or maybe I was the lesser of two evils; Jesse could've done even worse.

Momentarily, my phone started ringing again, but this time the caller I.D. read, "Jess." I answered, worrying a bit about how I was going to tell him that I got the job and he didn't.

"Hey," Jesse greeted.

"Um, hi."

"That Rita lady from Hollister just called me. Listen, if you want me to quit, I will, and then maybe she'll give you the job as a second choice."

"I- what?" I stammered. I felt guilty for not even briefly considering giving up the job for him.

"I got the job," he said with a hint of guilt.

I hesitated. "But Rita called me and said that she wanted to hire me."

"Wait... she called *me* and said she wanted to hire *me*."

I shrugged. "Well, I guess she wants to hire both of us."

"Yeah. That's awesome! Are you going on Monday at nine?"

I nodded, then facepalmed when I realized what I was doing.

"Yup. You too?"
"Uh huh. So I'll see you at work, I suppose."
"Yeah. See you."

That weekend went by slowly, as most of my summer had been. At last, Monday rolled around, and I was glad I had an excuse to get out of bed. However, I was not exactly thrilled with the notion of going to work at a clothing store.

Jesse and I spent the whole day learning the ins and outs of Hollister from a friendly redheaded employee, Erin. There wasn't a lot to know, so we ended up lazing about most of the day.

Erin was a grade below Jesse and I, which meant she was going into her senior year. An exciting time, if I remember correctly. But also, you know, terrifying. Deciding what you wanted to do with your life wasn't easy.

I remember spending hours mulling over majors and contemplating colleges. I also remember the immense relief I felt once I'd made the big decision to go into biology. It was also a great relief when I finally decided to follow Tate to the University of Illinois.

Erin still didn't know what she wanted to major in, or where she wanted to go.

The thing about Erin is that she was so nice and really pretty and I couldn't find anything not to like, but I still felt negatively towards her. It wasn't that a seething hatred grew in my heart, but I was aware of how great she was without feeling that she was all that great.

Maybe it was jealousy. Erin was carefree and had a laugh that sounded cute but not pathetic; she was everything I wasn't. I hardly remembered what it was like to be so innocent and not have to think about much besides school and what to wear.

Jesse did not seem to feel this instinctive dislike. He befriended Erin immediately. Which was good, because I was able to get away with barely talking. I stood back while Jesse and Erin passed the minutes in conversation.

While Erin was busy helping a gaggle of girls find the crop-tops they'd seen online, Jesse nudged me and whispered, "We can handle this, right? It'll all be worth it for Europe."

There were several European things on the bucket list. There was "Kiss a British guy" (no idea how Jesse planned on doing that one,) and there was also "Go to the top of the Eiffel Tower." Which, as lovely as it must've sounded to fourteen-year-old Tate, was an incredible inconvenience for eighteen-year-old me. "Yeah, it's not too bad," I relented.

That night was my first piano lesson with Edward Perkins. I met him at my church, which was where he taught his students. "Hi, Mr. Perkins," I greeted him with my biggest and best fake smile. For whatever reason, I was exceptionally nervous. The teacher didn't seem too menacing, though; he had graying hair and big rimmed glasses.

"You must be Leesie. And please, call me Ed."

The lesson went pretty much as I'd expected it to go. How can I put this? A platypus would be more talented at playing the piano than I was. At the beginning of the lesson, I told Ed that I played the ukulele. This seemed to give him the impression that I was musically inclined. I wasn't.

Ed was nice about it though, and encouraging. He was pretty weird but he was also a good teacher and appeared to be a piano expert. At the end of the lesson, he asked me, "Do you have a piano or keyboard at home?"

I nodded.

"Okay, that's magnificent. Practice what we've worked on as much as possible. Here." He handed me the sheet music to the simple song, "Gumball Factory," he'd decided would make a good first.

As I left, I handed him money for the lesson. "Ah, thank you dear. See you next week."

"Bye, thank you."

My life fell into a rhythm. Almost every morning, Jesse would pull up outside of my house and honk his horn, then I'd run outside and we'd carpool to Hollister. In the car we'd scheme about how to get the bucket list done before we went off our separate ways in August. We were trying to spend as much time as possible working, so that we could get enough money to finish the list.

Money was clearly no object to Tate, because not only did she want to go to Europe, she also had her sights set on California, New York, and Minnesota. She wanted to stand under the Hollywood sign and shop in New York and at the Mall of America. So Jesse and I worked everyday, like a drum beating to a steady rhythm.

However, I had the occasional interruption from this pattern. For example, when my mother dragged me to another visit with Dr. Señuarez. On the plus side, it was probably my last. On the minus side, well... how about I just tell you about it.

It started out as both of the others had, with Jenni asking me how I was doing. I was slightly more responsive than I'd been; I answered truthfully, with details. It was when I began telling her more about the bucket list that things went awry.

"Well, I've started taking piano lessons. And I'm working at Hollister now! Hopefully Jesse and I can raise enough money to be able to take on some of the travel-heavy things on the list."

"Why do you keep calling it '*the* list?' Why not 'my list?'" she burst out suddenly, dropping her therapist voice.

I didn't know how to respond. The question seemed so out of place. So abrupt. And her tone seemed sharp and accusatory. I began shaking my head, and mumbled, "I, uh..."

"It's because it's not your list, is it?" She stated bluntly, "It's Tate's."

After an extended moment of quiet, I demanded, "How did you know that?"

"It was just a guess. I knew that you and Jesse were never as close to each other as Tate. I also knew a few things Tate always wanted to do, things that seemed out of character for you to attempt. And she once mentioned that she had a bucket list."

"I didn't know you knew her so well."

Jenni seemed surprised. "Of course! I was her therapist. I saw her twice a week for over six months." Her eyes fell down to the table.

My mind raced. Why hadn't Tate ever told me she had a therapist? "Well clearly it didn't help much," I lashed.

The defeated-looking woman across from me didn't resemble the Jenni I'd thought I knew. My eyes prickled as I imagined being in her place: the therapist who couldn't help her patient.

Jenni slowly began, "I.. failed. All those sessions we had, I was trying to save her. But I'm a failure of a therapist. She's dead because of me."

"No, no! Look, I'm sorry. I shouldn't of said that. It's not true," I tried to console her.

"Don't try and tell me it isn't true!" she yelled, causing me to jump back in my seat. Then, with tears streaming down her face, she screamed, "Get out!" I didn't have to be told twice, so I frantically rushed out the door.

So that, dear readers, is how I finally got out of therapy for good.

- [x] Work at Hollister
- [x] Learn to play piano

☐ PARTY ALL NIGHT LONG

I managed to block out the therapy session enough to jump back into my routine. Before I knew it, three weeks had passed, I mastered the piano piece, and Jesse and I each had 750 dollars saved up. One day as we were in the car, I asked, "So when are we going to go to California?"

That Friday night, we stayed up late, planning how we would spend our money when we went to California. We had barely enough for a two night stay. We wanted to cross three different things off of the bucket list: "Stand under the Hollywood sign," "Learn to surf," and "Party all night long." Oh Tate, dearest Tate... why?

I have done a lot for Tate. I have done things I would never think of doing for anyone else. Convincing my parents to let me go to California with Jesse for two nights without supervision was among those things.

I'm not entirely sure how things worked out as perfectly as they did. Maybe my dad had heard Jesse and I scheming, and secretly knew about the bucket list. Maybe he simply had lots of misplaced trust in me. Or maybe he just didn't care.

I was sitting with my parents the next morning, eating toast, and I marveled something to the effect of, "How fun would it be to go to California?"

My mom made this "tsk tsk" sound as though I had asked,

"How fun would it to go to a strip club?" However, my dad responded, "Well, you and Jesse have been working very hard lately, maybe you guys should use the money you've earned to go on a road trip."

To this day, I'm not sure who was more surprised by this, my mom or I. I realized my mouth was hanging open and shut it. "Yeah! That'd be good. We could pool our money from Hollister. Great idea, Dad! I'll go call him right now!"

I jumped up and walked out of the kitchen with a spring in my step, pausing in the living room to eavesdrop on their conversation.

"You shouldn't encourage her with things like that. She should be saving up for college, not running off to Vegas with some boy," my mom scolded my dad.

"Honey, honey. This is Jesse. You and I both know he's gay." I tried not to laugh out loud, because Jesse was very much not gay, and also because my dad's tone suggested it was so obvious.

And then, my mom admitted, "Well, probably." I lost it at that, but luckily they didn't hear me.

"Also, isn't it so good to see her getting excited about something? After everything she's been through?" My mom couldn't argue with that, and I called Jesse to tell him (most of) the whole story.

So, we spent the next week fully preparing for the trip. It wasn't too tricky, with our parents' help. The thing about Jesse's mom is that she adored me, so if Jesse said he wanted to go somewhere with me, the answer was always yes. Even if it was California. Even if it was in her car.

It was a thirty hour drive. I had never been on a thirty hour drive, but I could imagine, and I was not looking forward to it. So when Jesse pulled into my driveway at five A.M. on Monday, I was actually not excited about going. But I hugged my parents goodbye and got into the little Mazda anyway.

It wasn't long before the hours began to blend together.

Sometimes, when neither of us could sleep, we'd listen to Mrs. Roe's CD's, which were all seventies and eighties music. Or else we'd talk, about the most random things. We actually discussed pickles at one point for a concerningly lengthy period of time. Seriously, our conversation revolved around pickles. For over an hour.

When we finally managed to get to LA, it was five o'clock on Tuesday. We decided to get checked in and sleep for a few hours before heading out to party.

Our hotel room was mangy and contained no colors except for brown. But, it would do. It had two beds and a TV, and honestly, that's all that we needed.

I fell asleep almost instantly; I was exhausted. When Jesse woke me up it was pitch black outside. "Let's get this over with," he sighed. If you couldn't tell, neither of us were the "party type."

It wasn't hard to find a party in Los Angeles; the tricky part was finding one that would let us in. See, we were both not invited and not of age, which made us poor partying candidates.

When we asked the guy at the front desk if he knew any good partying spots, he raised his eyebrows judgmentally but proceeded to list off some clubs nearby.

"I don't want to do this," I told Jesse as we stepped outside onto the sidewalk illuminated by streetlights overhead.

Our hotel was pretty far from the heart of the city, so we hopped on a bus and rode until the streets were really busy, eventually deciding we were close enough.

I was a good kid. I never lied to my parents or went to parties, or anything like that. But that was before I was thrust into Tate's shoes. And while I would consider Tate good, she wasn't well-behaved.

So Jesse and I followed a group of people into a club, and since we managed to absorb ourselves in with them, the guy at the door didn't I.D. us. Probably because he didn't notice us, but that's besides the point.

In the club, it was dark but also bright which doesn't make much sense. There were a lot of flashing lights and people. There was a constant beat going on... it was overwhelming to feel the whole place booming over and over and over and over again. I tried my best not to touch any strangers, which was nearly impossible, because there were so many people.

Jesse and I exchanged glances. After a moment, he shrugged, and pulled me over to the dance floor by the hand. The music was ear-splitting and the pulsing lights were giving me a headache, but I tried to have as much fun as possible.

After dancing for a while, I sat down in one of the chairs overlooking the dance floor. A few minutes later, Jesse appeared out of nowhere with two drinks in his hand. "What is this?" I shouted over the din.

"I don't know, some girly thing I thought Tate would've liked."

I tasted it. First, it tasted horrible. I scrunched up my face. Then, it tasted fruity for a second, and I thought it was actually pretty good, but then it went right back to tasting awful.

Jesse broke out into a grin. He chuckled. "Your face! This is what you looked like." He made a super ugly scrunched-up face, then switched to a sweet little smile, then went back to ugly.

"Well, that's what it tastes like!" I defended myself. Jesse laughed.

I found, however, that the more I drank it, the less revolting it tasted and the more similar to fruit punch it became. I also found that the more drinks I had, the more relaxed I was. Which led me to make the big mistake of drinking a lot.

I don't remember many details, either because I was too drunk or because I blocked them out afterwards, but I do remember music, dancing, and loud loud loud. It was so loud. So, at some point in the wee hours of the morning, I suggested to Jesse that we leave, because roaring music was giving me a headache.

Also, I remember kissing Jesse. Which I would beat myself up for later, both the kissing part and the remembering part. Of everything I forgot, why couldn't I have forgotten that?

I'm not sure exactly how it happened, but I remember kissing him, and thinking he was a good kisser. I also remember thinking, Tate won't care, she's dead. She chose to die. It's her fault I'm here instead of her. Which is a horrible thought and also untrue. Tate would probably never have been able to travel to California with Jesse. But I thought it. Then I made out with him. Oops.

I woke up sitting next to a building, in an alleyway. Jesse was sitting next to me, and my head was on his shoulder. I had a brief freak out moment when I remembered what happened.

I jumped up and took a few big steps away from him. My movement caused him to wake up too. He also jumped up. "Let's get out of here," was all I said. The problem was we couldn't quite decide where "here" was. And my phone was dead. And his phone was dead.

Directly out of the alley, we came to a road we'd never seen before. Cars were driving by and it was annoyingly bright. As I scrutinized every which way we could, struggling to find something even remotely recognizable, my hope of escape died.

"Let's uh... that way," I pointed in a direction that seemed to be a good idea.

"You know it's that way?" Jesse asked.

"Nope. I, like yourself, have never been to Los Angeles," I contended rather crankily.

About five minutes or so of dawdling around, what I was dreading was affirmed. "Leesie... did I have a, uh, dream last ni..." his voice slowly died as I shook my head while we continued to aimlessly roam. "Right. Okay then." In his infinite wisdom, Jesse decided to drop the subject for good.

"Look at us, two drunks trying to find their way home from an alleyway in a city they don't know," I declared. "What happened to me?!"

"Yeah, didn't expect to ever have this going on," Jesse mumbled.

I shot him an accusing glance. "It was you who got us those drinks, you know."

He raised his hands up in defense, and I thought he was going to continue, but apparently not. I turned my head away and continued walking. He sighed. "Suddenly this feels very real."

"Never had a hangover, Jesse?" I questioned ironically.

"No, no. This." He waved his arms around above his head and frankly looked kind of crazy. "The bucket list."

He did have a point. Weeks now, it had been little things. A piano lesson, sleeping in a hand-built treehouse, marathoning the sappiest love story on the planet. And now we were in California, because of a single sheet of paper a friend wrote years ago. A friend that wasn't even there to see us.

"If I hadn't taken it from her room," I began, "none of this would've happened."

"Yeah, I guess you're right."

I remained silent for a few moments. "I mean, it was an afterthought. Something I took because I didn't know what else to take. Some tiny little thing that changed everything." We turned onto a new street, but this one was as unfamiliar as the last. "What if there was some tiny little thing back then? Something that could've changed things."

"What do you mean?" Jesse inquired.

"Something that could've saved her. But I didn't even notice it and now she's dead." It came out a lot harsher than I'd expected it to.

"Leesie, I mean, come on. That's nothing but a superstition. Even if there was, it doesn't matter and there's no point dwelling on it," he asserted.

"So I should move on, right? Forget about her and get on with my life, because it's been so long since it happened and I'm being an overly-emotional teenage girl?" I spat.

"Nobody actually thinks that, right?" Jesse asked with disbelief in his voice.

I grumbled, "More than you'd think."

"Hmm…" Jesse murmured in response. I waited a good minute

for him to continue.

"What?" I finally burst out.

"Nothing, it's just... people think you should forget? And that's how you move on, by forgetting?"

"Guess so," I responded blatantly.

"That doesn't make sense."

"Why not?" I questioned, genuinely confused. It was a motif between people, a way to try and comfort somebody who'd lost something. You make them feel better by telling them to try to forget about it.

"Why would anyone want to move on in their life by forgetting what they've lost? That's as bad as running away," Jesse stated. "I want to move on with Tate. Not from Tate."

"She's gone, Jesse. How would you go about doing that?" But he didn't have to answer. I realized what he was saying moments after I spoke. Because moving on with Tate was exactly what we were there to do.

☑ Party all night long

☐ LEARN TO SURF

*Tate pulled out her hardwood chair and slowly sat down, avoiding all eye contact with her parents. She didn't want to ignite another argument with them, not after what had happened when they'd first found out. She was probably in the clear though; neither of them had spoken to her in days. Not anything real, anyway.

"Tate, could you pass you the salt?"

"Yes," she responded automatically, moving the salt across the dinner table to her mother.

"Thank you."

"You're welcome." Tate bent her head and stared down at her plate. She had almost gotten used to the shunning, the awkwardness, the constant reminder that she'd been abandoned. A horrible, disgusting, pitiful sort of used to.

Not pulling her eyes away from her dinner, Tate said timidly, "Would it be alright if I met a friend at the park tonight?"

"Oh, him? Yes, you may. We didn't expect anything different," Tate's dad said coldly, sending a dagger through her already punctured heart.

"Thank you..." Tate tried to say, but her voice got caught in her throat.

Later, when she was about to leave, she called into the house, "Bye," but got nothing in response. *Oh well*, she thought to herself. *I won't have to deal with this for much longer.*

Los Angeles was a maze. And I'll tell you, Jesse and I were not very good at being mice.

When we finally reached the hotel, following the directions of a kindly old bus driver, we both collapsed onto our beds. "Ugh..." I groaned. "So tired." My head was throbbing. My legs felt like lead from wandering around.

"You'll be happy to know that we're going surfing today." Jesse's voice dripped with sarcasm.

"Why?" I whined.

"Already reserved lessons at three o'clock. Nonrefundable."

"Ick... What time is it?" I whined as I covered my face with a pillow so no light could reach my retinas.

"It's eleven. And it takes twenty minutes to get there."

"Do you have any good news?!" I yelled into my pillow.

Jesse chuckled. "I'll wake you at 2:00."

"2:15." I hurled a pillow at his face to let him know I meant it.

When the hour of reckoning came I was feeling slightly more up to spec. Keyword: slightly. However, since the idea of surfing had always enticed me, there was excitement to go along with my pain and nausea.

The excitement grew when we arrived at a beautiful beach. And it grew again when we met our instructor, a cute surfer guy with blond hair and strong arms.

"Hey, I'm Cory," he introduced himself in an adorable Australian accent. "You two look like naturals."

We laughed, and I kept praying that he was right as he explained what we were going to do. However, the more Cory instructed us, the more difficult surfing sounded.

"I know it sounds tough here on sand, mate," Cory said to Jesse, "but once we get in the water it'll just happen. You'll see."

"What if it doesn't?" Jesse asked, unconvinced.

"I will not get out of the water until both of you have caught at least one wave. Now, come on, let's get in."

The moment my feet touched the cold ocean, the memories of the last time I had stood in salty water washed over me like the waves that lapped against my ankles. Before high school, I would always go up and spend a week at Tate's beach house with her in the summer. The cool breeze, the endless sound of waves, and the best friend in the whole world made those weeks the highlight of not only my summer, but my life.

I looked out at the horizon, recalling the days we'd spent splashing around, or simply resting by letting the waves carry us in and out and in and out again.

We were powerless to the ocean, just like we were powerless to emotion. I suppose Tate had forgotten to let the waves carry her back in. So now I was alone, standing in the shallows, scanning the surface of the depths, knowing deep down she could never find her way to the sunlight.

"Come on, guys, it's not too bad," Cory called out, snapping me back to reality.

"It's freezing!" Jesse exclaimed, but nonetheless began wading deeper, to where Cory stood with the three boards floating around him. We hopped on the boards, and began what the most generous of souls might have called surfing.

Jesse and I were not naturals. In fact, we were the farthest from naturals we could be. Cory kept laughing at us (yes, we were that bad) but I didn't mind, because he was really handsome when he laughed.

He kept true to his word, though, and he wouldn't let us leave until we each successfully surfed a wave. When I finally got up at around 5:30, I think all three of us were relieved to finally escape the salty prison of the ocean.

When, at last, I collapsed on the dry sand, exhaustion and the need for a drink overcame everything else. Honestly, the only thought crossing my mind was *water water food water water!*

After my appetite had been satisfied by the local deli and my thirst quenched by some bottled "mountain spring" water from the "Himalayas," I took a moment to fully appreciate that we had just crossed one more thing off of Tate's bucket list. Check.

As we walked up the path, I mused, "I can't believe we're leaving today."

"Yeah. It's been fun."

I laughed. "At least the parts we remember were."

"Yeah," he agreed with a chuckle.

"You know, one thing I do remember from our partying is your... intriguing dance moves."

"Intriguing?" Jesse raised an eyebrow.

"Well, yeah, like... the crabwalk? What exactly was that?"

"Hey, sorry! Last time I went to a dance was eighth grade. Alone," Jesse informed.

"Ooh."

Jesse was silent.

I was silent.

Finally, I mumbled, "Sorry."

After a moment, Jesse broke into a laugh and I couldn't help but follow.

"But wait, what about when you were dating that one lacrosse girl?" I asked.

"Emily? Well, we were together during homecoming but her leg was broken. And we broke up before prom came around."

"Aw, that sucks," I said, for lack of anything better to say.

Jesse looked at me. "Well..." he started, smiling a little. "It wasn't *too* hard on me."

Our conversation was cut short as we approached the chain-link fence that blocked us from the Hollywood sign.

We couldn't actually get under the sign, which was sad, because the list specifically said to stand under it. However, we could get behind it, which in my opinion was even cooler.

THE BUCKET LIST

We were silently standing there, both staring at it, when Jesse turned to me. So, I turned to him. I expected him to speak. He didn't speak. He did, however, lean in ever so slowly. Once I realized what was going on, I was shocked, and instinctively slapped him.

His reaction was not what I expected. He nodded, pressed his lips together, and murmured, "Thought so."

- ☑ Learn to surf
- ☑ Stand under the Hollywood sign

☐ HAVE A PAINT FIGHT

There's nothing quite like locking two people in a car for thirty hours to cure a kink in their relationship. Before even an hour had passed, all the awkwardness had dissipated; Jesse and I were back to normal.

We tried to plan during the abundant hours of the drive, but it was hard to get anything concrete figured out. We decided to wait until we had some money saved up before we started planning any more travel. Until then, we'd simply work as much as possible to build up our funds.

That plan sounded great when we talked about it, but in real life it sucked. Working at Hollister wasn't hard, but it did take a bit of brainpower and a significant amount of time. Also, it required talking to a bunch of preteens who thought they were so cool for shopping there.

Needless to say, I was getting to know my co-workers well. Along with Erin and Jesse, there was a guy named Todd. He had dyed black hair and alternative-style clothes, and always wore spike bracelets. I'll admit, at first, he kind of scared me. But after getting to know him, I discovered he was actually a cool guy with a passion for baking. Sometimes he even brought me cookies, which were so melty and delectable that they almost made working bearable. Almost.

The Hollister life was one I had never expected to live. It could've been it's own little sitcom, starring Leesie Derell and Jesse Roe, with supporting actors Erin and Todd. Orders being mixed up, time-tables being inaccurate, and drama between the four protagonists were among some of the many things that kept our audience coming back week in and week out.

One Saturday, during an episode featuring only Jesse and I, we were sorting through a bunch of new clothes that had recently been shipped in. I was three boxes in to an intense shirt-folding marathon, and was not in the least thinking about what Jesse was doing, when he ran up to me frantically. "Leesie, Leesie, Leesie!" he bellowed, even though we were a foot apart.

"What?"

Jesse held up a pink flowery sundress. "I found my perfect dress!"

Laughing, I rolled my eyes. One of the things on the bucket list was finding the perfect dress.

Jesse ran over to the cash register, shoved ten dollars in it, and declared, "Yes! It's mine!"

"You're seriously going to buy it?"

His face fell. "What? You don't like it?"

The truth was, I liked it a lot. But I wasn't sure that that made it okay that Jesse was actually purchasing a dress. "I love it, it's just... well, you know, you'll never wear it."

Jesse scrunched up his nose, and became immersed in thought. "True, true," he agreed after a minute. "Here, you can have it. You'd look prettier in it than I would."

I had another piano lesson with Mr. Perkins that night. The thing about Mr. Perkins is that he loved piano. Really loved it. Perkins loved piano the way kids in commercials love toys. He was so giddy about it, and his enthusiasm made me excited as well.

On that particular night, Mr. Perkins was teaching me how to play the chords to "You Are My Sunshine." It was funny, because he'd sing along in different voices and I'd burst out laughing while still trying to play. It was exhausting.

By the time I got to bed that night, I was beat. And whenever I was exhausted, I made the mistake of letting my guard down, letting my thoughts roam around in my mind. I tried not to think about Tate as much as possible, but sometimes, as I lay in bed, I wondered why she did it. And recently, I'd been thinking about it more often.

I couldn't understand why the girl I thought I knew so well went off and proved me so wrong. And as time passed, my confusion faded into anger.

Being mad at her hardly helped, but it helped a bit. And when the mind is shrouded in darkness, it'll grab on to the first light it sees.

I had known she was depressed. Her parents knew too, and her doctor. She was on some weird antidepressant that was supposed to help, but didn't seem to. What I never managed to figure out was why she had become so sad in the first place. I know that depression can be seemingly random and without a cause, but I refused to believe that my best friend had killed herself over nothing.

Tate's depression started near the end of our junior year, about a year before the suicide. Something bad happened with her school friends, but she wouldn't tell me what it was. And then, one by one, they stopped talking to her.

I tried to talk to her at school as much as possible, but we had no classes together, different lunch periods, and our lockers were at opposite ends of the school. Plus, Tate at school was constantly grouchy. Soon Tate became that way outside of school too.

Yet, I never knew what the event prompted the change was. And it bugged me. It's not as though I wanted to avenge her or anything, I just wanted to know.

So I decided something. The next day, I wasn't working, not because I didn't want to work, but because Jesse and Erin had taken all of the shifts. This gave me time, which I decided to spend searching for an answer.

I wasn't sure where to start, so I ended up going to see Tate's friend Taylor. Taylor was a gorgeous popular girl. She was one of

Tate's best school friends before those friends started estranging her. I was hoping she could answer some of my questions.

So I showed up at her house, and rang the doorbell. I probably should've called first, but the problem was, I didn't have her number. But I did know where she lived, because of one unfortunate evening when Tate dragged me to a party there.

Soon Taylor opened the door. "Leesie?" Frankly, I was impressed that she recognized me.

"Hi."

"Hi." Taylor forced a smile. "Come in, come in."

Her house had this weird thing about it: even though it had lots and lots of expensive-looking windows, it was dark.

"I was wondering if you'd be willing to talk to me about Tate. About why she..." I trailed off.

"Um. Yeah, sure," Taylor agreed. "Tea?"

Despite modern Disney movies' assurance otherwise, I have discovered that some popular people are actually nice. I decided that Taylor was one of them. I nodded, and she led me into her kitchen.

After a few minutes, I asked, "So what do you think made Tate so depressed?"

Before answering, Taylor gave me a mug of steaming hot tea and plopped down in a chair across the table from me. "Well, I guess Brad started it," Taylor stated while biting her nails.

"Brad? Brad Shager?" Brad was the quarterback at our highschool, and Tate and I had always thought he was a jerk. Then, for who-knows-what reason, she started dating him. Only for a few weeks, but still, I never understood why she'd even think of going out with him.

"Yeah. When they broke up."

"But she broke up with him."

Taylor stared at me for a moment. "Well, technically, yeah. But only because he cheated on her."

When I had processed the new information enough to move on,

I said, "Okay... I guess you better tell me the whole story from the beginning."

"Okay. Alright. Okay." She bit her thumb nail again, with more ferocity. She quickly glanced behind her, as if making sure nobody was eavesdropping. "So, spring break junior year, Molly Andrews had this huge party. And Tate came." Tate had invited me to that party. I had refused to go because, at the time, I had been nurturing the belief that popular people didn't have souls.

Taylor continued, "And Brad was there. Some of our friends were telling Tate to go talk to him, and so she did. About a week later they started dating. Do you know Sophie Nives?"

I was slightly taken aback by this seemingly unrelated question, but I did know Sophie (or at least knew of her,) so I nodded.

"Well, a few weeks after Tate and Brad start dating, Tate goes to surprise him at some random football practice, and she sees Sophie and Brad making out."

"Whoa." Sophie used to be one of Tate's closest friends. That was cold.

"Yeah. So I'm guessing that's what started it," Taylor concluded. "Oh, and most of Tate's friends were also Sophie's friends and they sided with Sophie." Taylor glanced down for a minute, then spoke softly to the table. "Including me, for a bit."

"Was that it though?" I asked. It didn't seem like enough to drive Tate to take such drastic measures.

Taylor snapped her head up, and seemed a bit offended when she answered, "Tate took it really hard."

She seemed to be getting rather upset... perhaps it was time for me to make my way out.

I stood up. "Thanks, Taylor," I concluded our brief 'reunion' as we began walking to the entryway.

"No problem. See you around, maybe."

I smiled a bit. "Yup. Thanks again! Bye."

The following day, I didn't have work again, so I had nothing to do. Which really meant I had Netflix to do. I was totally immersed in the second season of a show I'd started that day when my phone buzzed with a text from Jesse. He was just saying hi, and since I was preoccupied with my show, I ignored it.

A few hour later, he texted me again.

Jess: *Come outside*

Me: *But I'm comfy.*

Jess: *Come*

I dragged myself out of bed, down the stairs, and through the front door. Jesse was standing in the middle of the yard. "Come on," he shouted to me, and gestured for me to come over to him.

With a sigh, I trudged out to where he stood. My lack of enthusiasm didn't seem to bother him though. He smiled brightly and handed me a bottle of green tempera paint.

"What?" I questioned, but took it nonetheless.

"How do you feel about the clothes you're wearing?"

I gazed down, completely baffled, and contemplated my sweatpants and old t-shirt. Jesse took in my outfit, and I figured answering was unnecessary.

"Okay, let's begin."

"Begin what?" I queried, but before I had even finished, Jesse uncapped his paint and splattered me with it. And that's when I remembered that having a paint fight was one of the things on the bucket list.

Within seconds, paint was flying through the wind, as two forces battled the battle of a century.

At some point during the war, my dad returned home from work. Jesse stopped to say hi to him, which was a huge mistake on his part. I was able to go for the sneak attack and I managed to splatter him with the rest of my paint. Unfortunately, some of the paint that missed Jesse sloshed onto my father's pants. He ogled at me, and I froze. Ever so slowly, he shook his head, and, without speaking, walked inside.

As soon as the door swung shut behind him, Jesse and I both started laughing. "Seriously?!" he exclaimed. "I was clearly on a time out."

"All is fair in love and war," I said brightly.

"So be it," he stated, and in one swift motion dumped the rest of his paint over my head.

Cold paint soaked through my hair and reached my scalp. "Oh my gosh Jesse you did not just do that!" I was out of paint, but that didn't stop me from chasing him around the yard until I had a stitch in my side.

☑ Have a paint fight

☐ GO GOTH FOR A DAY

We sat in my yard under the big tree while the sun set, talking about plans and the bucket list.

"So what's next?" Jesse asked at one point.

I shrugged. "I don't know. What do you want to do next?"

"You're working tomorrow, right?"

"Yeah."

Jesse laughed to himself. "Let's go goth."

I facepalmed. I was so mad at Tate for putting that on the list. "We'll get fired."

"No we won't. It's just one day. But I'm going to need your help with makeup. How about I come over at nine, and we can car pool?"

I thought about his plan. And I thought about my black eye liner. "Fine, but you're going to have to stop by Walgreens or something beforehand to pick up some black lipstick. It's essential."

"Alright," Jesse agreed. Then he repeated to himself, "Be here, tomorrow, by nine, with the lipstick."

"Right. I should go shower." I touched my head, where there was still wad of crusted paint.

Jesse nodded, and inspected the paint covering him. "Okay. Me too." He stood up and started to walk home. "Goodnight," he called.

"Goodnight."

The next morning, Jesse rang my doorbell (at exactly nine, of course.) In his hands he held not only the black lipstick, but also stick-on nose rings and tons of studded bracelets.

"You came prepared, as usual," I commented.

Jesse shrugged it off.

We spent a little more than half of an hour getting decked out and goth-looking. When Jesse was done, I barely recognized him. I had made him brush his black hair down over one of his eyes, which were rimmed with thick strokes of black eyeliner. He wore ripped black skinny jeans that he'd borrowed from his little brother Graham, and a plain black t-shirt.

I was much less impressed with myself. I simply couldn't pull the style off, at least not without dying my hair much darker. And that was not on the table. I did give a good attempt at going goth though, and that counted for something.

When we arrived at work, Rita was there unlocking. She stared at us for several moments with her head cocked, then nodded. "Okay. I'm not even going to ask. But you should be wearing clothes from the store. Here, borrow these for today." She grabbed two leather jackets off of a rack and handed them to us.

We accepted, and the rest of the day went without a hitch. Sure, the shopping teenage girls gave us quite a few weird looks, but I got used to it. Besides, the judgmental reactions from various customers were all worth it to see Todd's reaction to us donning his personal style; he couldn't stop smiling.

That was the day that we started seriously talking about our trip to Europe. In order to finish the bucket list, we had to A) kiss a British boy and B) go to the top of the Eiffel Tower. Money was our main obstacle, and our second was our parents.

By this point, my parents had picked up that Jesse and I were on some type of quest, but they didn't know that it had to do with Tate. We were about to go off to college, so it would make sense that we would try to do lots of fun activities that we'd always wanted to do, for instance going to Cali.

However, I figured that convincing them to permit (and cofund) my transcontinental travel would be a new challenge.

The problem with Europe is that it costs a lot to go there. So, we were trying to think of ideas to make it less expensive. "If we could get more people to come with us, we could split costs with them," Jesse suggested.

"Yeah, but who?" I asked.

He shrugged. We were both quiet for a minute while we thought.

I broke the silence. "Maybe we could stay with someone we know? Do you know anyone in England or France?"

Jesse looked dismayed. "No... you?"

"Well, Ella had a French foreign exchange student junior year, but I don't know her well enough to stay with her."

Jesse's eyes lit up. "I have an idea! It solves both problems. We invite Ella, split costs with her, and that way we can stay with her foreign exchange student."

I raised one eyebrow. "You barely know Ella. Wouldn't that be weird? Plus, we're sort of using her then."

"No, no. It'd be fine," he assured, as if that cleared up all of my concerns. "She'd love it. And we're tight." He held up his hand and crossed his fingers to indicate their apparent tightness. I scoffed, and our conversation was interrupted by a bunch of brawny boys who wanted to check out.

While Jesse was helping them, I texted Ella about the trip. When my phone dinged a while later, I expected it to be a text from Ella, but it was actually from Maddie.

Jesse was the one who made me go. Had I been given a fair choice, I wouldn't have gone. I tramped up the porch steps and knocked on the minty green door. The thought I had previously had when I was on those steps recurred to me, that perhaps it was the last time I'd ever be standing there. I began to chuckle dryly, as if it was a crude joke. I could never escape Tate.

Maddie had invited me over again, to clean out Tate's room. I would've stayed home, if Jesse hadn't forced me to do otherwise.

Maddie came to the door wearing an apron with her hair tied back, an unusual appearance for her. "Hi Leesie." She beamed at me and stepped out of the way so I could walk inside. "I'm so glad you came!"

I fake-smiled back. "Of course." But in my mind I was thinking, *If Jesse hadn't made me come, I wouldn't be here.* I was there, however, so I tried to accept that fact and move on.

She started going up the stairs, and I followed. "All of this is going to be donated, so if you want any of it please feel free to take it." She gestured to some bags in the loft.

Before I could respond, Mr. Conscivit, Tate's dad, came out of his room. He paused a second, peering through Tate's open door, then turned his attention to us. "Hello Leesie!" he exclaimed in a way that was surely supposed to sound cheery, but I could see the defeat written all over him.

"Hi, Mr. Conscivit," I replied.

After our greetings, he proceeded down the stairs and into the computer room, shutting the door behind him. After watching him the whole way, I turned to Maddie. She was still staring at the door he'd disappeared behind.

After a long moment, she spoke. "He would be helping us today, but..." She paused, then continued, "Well, he was the one who found her, you know."

I didn't know that, but I nodded anyway.

"He hasn't been in there. It's bad for me, and I can only imagine how bad it is for him."

"That's awful," I whispered.

Maddie nodded. "But we'll get through it. It will make things a lot easier once we clean the room out."

In my mind, I wondered if that was true. A memory flashed into my mind of a conversation Jesse and I had had while wandering the streets of California. It sounded to me like Maddie was trying to move on from Tate, not with her. I kept my mouth shut though. People have to pick their own battles.

Maddie listed off a few things that were to be saved, and the rest I was supposed sort into bags for either donating or throwing away. Tate's homework and school related papers were what I gathered first, to toss. Then, we collected all her blankets, pillows, and sheets.

Underneath her *5 Seconds of Summer* pillow I found a small gray sheet of plastic. After throwing the pillow into the donation pile, I picked the plastic up to examine further. It was one of those sheets doctors give you, with pills inside of little clear pouches. And every single pouch had been popped.

"Hey, Maddie?" She glanced up from across the room. "What's this from?"

Maddie strolled over and took the plastic, examining it. "No need to keep this. Probably from her antidepressants," she responded, before casually tossing it into the throw away pile.

That sounded fine to me, until about an hour later I went to the bathroom. As I was searching the cupboard for soap, I found a small orange medicine bottle. The label consisted of Tate's name, some fancy sounding words, followed by "antidepressant." So it wasn't in little pouches?

I ended up shrugging it off, though; I had other things to think about besides the plethora of medications Tate was taking to wield off her ever-present depression. It's not like they did anything anyway.

The rest of the day passed with much bagging and sorting, and I didn't leave until 4:30. As we were standing in the entryway, Maddie said to me, "Thank you so much for your help, Leesie. I don't know what I would've done without you." After a second, she added, "I don't know what Tate would've done without you."

In my mind, I thought, *Maybe she wouldn't have died,* but out loud, I simply replied, "You're welcome." *Perhaps,* I thought, as I walked out of the house, *I'm walking out of the Conscivit's lives forever.* I hoped so.

☑ Go goth for a day

☐ KISS A BRITISH GUY

I devised a plan, an epic plan, that I would use to convince my parents. Ninety-nine percent foolproof. Leesie Derell guaranteed.

One morning, I was sitting in the kitchen with my parents, while they both read "The Daily Batavian." I had my laptop in front of me, and I was scrolling through the lovely social trap that is Facebook. Suddenly, I burst out, "No way!" This got both my mother and father to look up questioningly.

"Jake, Noah Hinsley, and Chris Simons are going on a trip together, because it's their last summer before they split up to go to college," I lied. There was no justification for that, other than the reasons I'd been using to justify most of the things from Tate's bucket list.

"That sounds fun," my dad answered and turned back to his newspaper.

Before he could become reabsorbed, I added, "I wish I was going on a trip with my friends."

My mother raised her eyebrows. "You've already gone to California with Jesse."

I sighed. "Yeah, that's true. I suppose I've lived enough." Then, before they could correct my pitiful comment, I added excitedly, "They're going to Greece and Italy, and all over the rest of Europe! Sick!"

Barely containing my grin, I got up and left the room. Sick? What was I thinking. Oh well, the rest had gone perfectly. Phase one: complete.

The next evening, after work, I strolled into the kitchen where my mom was stirring a pot of soup. I greeted, "Salut maman, ca va?"

She stared at me blankly. "Are you speaking French?"

I nodded. "I've heard that you can forget languages really fast. So, I want to keep in practice in case I ever get the opportunity to go to France."

My mom didn't say anything. After a minute, I added, "No, you're right, that's unrealistic. France is expensive; I could never get that much from Hollister alone." I sighed animately. "Oh well. I guess those four years were for nothing. Au revoir, maman."

I left the room, but waited right outside the door. When I peeked back in a minute later, my mom was still standing at the stove, stirring the soup, with a facial expression of slight bewilderment.

Phase two: complete.

Later that night, when I went down into the basement to practice piano, I found my dad sitting on the couch. Upon further inspection, I saw that he was watching some British show he watched a lot.

"Hey, Dad," I greeted. He paused the show, and it pulled up a bar that showed how far into the episode he was, with the title of the show right above it. I was struck by a sudden idea. "Oh my gosh, I love *Doctor Who*, it's basically my favorite show!" I exclaimed, maybe a little *too* enthusiastically.

"You've gotta be kidding me! Leese, how have we never bonded over this?!" my dad shouted.

"I don't know!" I squealed, and my father and I broke out into full-fledged fangirling. It mainly consisted with my dad raving about one thing, and then me rephrasing it and delivering it in a even more excited tone.

"Ahh, want to watch with me?" he asked after toning it down a little. "It's 'Blink!'"

"'Blink?!' OMG!" (yes, I verbally said OMG.) "Sorry, Dad, I'm rewatching in order, and I'm not where you are yet."

"No worries, Leese, I feel you." I was a bit shocked by him using that phrase. I must've found something he really loved. "'Blink' is probably too scary for you, anyway, isn't it?"

"Yeah..." I agreed, not quite sure what I was affirming.

"I love the scary episodes though. It's my favorite aspect of the show."

I nodded, discerning my segway. "My favorite is the Britishness. The accents, the locations. It's almost like I'm there. It's just... it's my childhood, Dad." Throughout my monologue, he nodded in agreement.

After a weighted pause, I continued, "The thing is, growing up, I always wanted to see England for myself. And now that my childhood is practically over, it's more or less my last chance. It's now or never, you know?"

My dad nodded, "Yeah, Leesie. Yeah..."

"But I guess it's going to be never, because it's clearly not going to happen now."

My father's only response was a stunned silence. I shrugged and walked back upstairs, forgetting to practice piano at all.

Phase three: Complete.

Up in my room that night, I was feeling guilty for lying to my dad. As a solution, I marathoned half of the first season of Dr. Who. I enjoyed it a lot, and proceeded to follow about ten Dr. Who fan blogs on Tumblr.

I would've watched more, but by that point, it was one in the morning. I had to work the next day (technically, that day,) so I decided it was best for me to get some sleep. But, sleep I didn't. My mind was too busy thinking about Europe, Raxacoricofallapatorians, and of course Tate.

At about three in the morning, I abandoned all hope of falling asleep, and decided to give Jesse a call. Being human, he was probably not awake, but being Jesse, he was most likely willing to talk to me no matter what the hour.

"It's rather early," he greeted, sounding only slightly groggy.

I grinned, "Hello to you too."

"Why you callin'?" he inquired.

"Can't sleep. Well, gave up on sleeping. And I'm bored now."

"Well, thank you for choosing Jesse Roe Boredom-Conquering Services. I promise you won't be disappointed."

I laughed more than I should've at that, probably because of my lack of sleep. When I'd calmed down, I said, "So, I became a Whovian tonight."

He gleefully exclaimed, "Welcome to the family!" as if I'd just announced my engagement to his son. Once again, I cracked up for far too long.

Finally, I answered with a simple, "Thanks."

"You're welcome. Speaking of *Doctor Who*, a British guy took my order at McDonalds yesterday. Not that you should kiss him, after ten minutes of conversation I figured out he's *totally* high maintenance. Speaking of British people, how's your Europe situation working out? Your parents diggin'?"

I couldn't help but giggle again. I was liking late night Jesse. "Ahh, well I devised a plan and phases three of four are complete. I'll need you for the next part. Becoming a Whovian was sort of a byproduct, but I think it's going quite well. It's only a matter of time before they say yes." The way I described the whole ordeal made me sound sort of like a Bond villain, but I think I got my point across.

"Well, you know how it is at my place. If you can go, I can go," Jesse affirmed. "What about Ellie?"

"Ella," I corrected. "And she's still pending, but her parents aren't easy to convince. At least, so I've heard."

"Say we all manage to get permission," Jesse began, "what do we do? What's the plan? It's one thing to drive to Cali, but this is a different continent. We'll need an idea of what we're going to do."

"Well, let's plan it out then. Perhaps we show Ella the treehouse," I suggested, with the hint of a smile in my voice.

"Perhaps we do. Tomorrow?" Jesse proposed.

"Tomorrow," I agreed. Something happened then: Jesse and I kept talking, for a good hour and a half. Not about the bucket list. Not about Europe, or Tate. Just talked about us. And it was nice.

"Welcome to our maison de l'arbre." Jesse presented the treehouse to Ella as it came into sight.

She gave a confused look. "Why the French?"

"We're going to France, and I need to be able to charm the natives," Jesse declaimed.

I rolled my eyes. "So you've decided that learning phrases such as 'tree house' will be useful? At what occasion would you *ever* say 'maison de l'arbre' other than if you were at a treehouse?"

Jesse smugly responded, "Smalltalk. Anyways, it's time we draw out the plans."

The three of us ascended the ladder we'd built into the tree.

The treehouse had been the best place for planning all things bucket list. I'm not sure why, but we always came up with the best ideas when we were sitting high in the branches. It was sort of like the bucket list gave it to us, as a gift. That sort of makes it sound like a vengeful deity that makes Jesse and me do it's bidding, but you get the point.

As we reached the top, Jesse turned to me. "So, Leesie, have your parents been persuaded yet?"

"Um..." I hesitated. "I'm working on it."

He shook his head disapprovingly at me. "How about you, Ella?"

"My parents said I could, and they'd match what I pay, as long as I mow the-"

"Wait, what?!" I cut in. "You got them to agree? How?"

"They saw the logic in my argument. After all, it is our last summer together. And this trip is the perfect way to end with a bang and make sure we stay friends during college and have tons of great memories to look back on."

Jesse gave me a glance, and I began to say, "Well, see, there's one other reason we're going to Europe..."

"Oh, okay. What is it?" Ella questioned.

I decided that it would be best to show her first, and explain after. I removed the folded up bucket list from my pocket and handed it to her. After she read it, she gave me a confused look.

"It was Tate's. I found it when I was over there, and I... we've been doing everything on her list." I proceeded to point out the European related bullet points to her. "We haven't told anybody about it. It's sort of a sensitive subject. But you're my friend. My best friend, now, I suppose."

Anyone else would have become uncomfortable hearing me say that. But Ella was different. "Then let's make sure we can all go to Europe and pay her the respect she deserves." Ella smiled.

"But, you're cool with that?" Jesse asked. He explained, "While we're there we have to do some things for the list that may seem odd, just so you know."

"Sure, why not?" Ella said good-naturedly.

Jesse nodded, the corners of his mouth curving up a bit. "You have really pretty eyes, by the way."

Ella blushed a little, then looked down. I raised my eyebrows, not sure what to think. Ella did have pretty eyes, one was hazel and the other was blue, but it seemed so odd for Jesse to say something about it.

However, the moment dissipated when Jesse continued, "Now, my parents have already said yes, as long as you can go," he turned to me. "Which means, it's down to you, Leese."

"Thanks for not putting any pressure on me," I replied sarcastically.

"Assuming Leesie uses the persuasion skills she has to the max and gets an affirmative, we need an agenda."

"And we need to map out our budget," Ella added.

The two of them jabbered on for a few minutes, with my occasional input. I'm not going to lie, they made a good team, planning out our trip to Europe as if it were a picnic.

When they had it all figured out, they filled me in. "So, we fly to London, and stay there four days. Then, we'll take a train to Paris, and stay there for three," Jesse explained. I nodded.

"And we'll stop in New York on the way home, to shop," Ella finished.

"That sounds great, but will we have enough money for it?"

Ella nodded. "If our parents pay half, and we use all that we have saved, yeah, just about the perfect amount."

I laughed. "Great life plan: lose all the money our parents saved for our education, but get a few nights in Europe instead!"

The other two laughed, and Ella pleaded, as though mocking herself, "But mom, I need life experiences before I go into the real world!"

This was followed by Jesse imitating himself, "Leesie's mom agreed to blowing it all on Europe. If she said yes, you *know* it's a good idea!"

I was left with no choice but to show them a scene from the epic drama of my plan. "Too bad all my years in high school French will be wasted; I'll never get to see the place of my dreams."

We all burst out laughing, and didn't stop for a long time. "You know," Jesse concluded finally, "this is going to be fun."

Jesse craned to look up at my mom, who was reading peacefully on the balcony above my front door. "Evening, Mrs. Derell!" I hung back, behind the corner of the house, to avoid being seen.

She lifted up her sunglasses to verify the greeter, then smiled. "Hi Jesse-boy!" We all found ourselves nearly vomiting upon hearing the title 'Jesse-boy' leaving her lips. She obviously had not thought the name through; she turned bright red with embarrassment. It passed quickly, however.

"Oh and hi... Ella?" she said, noticing Ella skipping alongside Jesse on the sidewalk in front of my house.

Around the corner, I could see Ella give back a sweet little wave, and do a sort of skipping thing to show she was happy. I'd seen better actresses, myself not included. My mom asked, "What are you two up to?"

"You'll never guess, Mrs. Derell. We're going to Europe!" Jesse exclaimed, leaping up in sync with Ella to exchange high-fives. "Couple nights in London, couple nights in Paris, pit stop in New York. It's going to be *great!*"

"Ahh!" Ella shrieked for effect.

My mother, still cooling down from the embarrassment, was having trouble taking the information in. "Well, that's great! When do you-" my mom was cut off as I emerged from behind the corner, right on cue, looking depressed. I slouched right through my two friends, bumping shoulders with them as they looked at me with concerned expressions. Finally, I made it to the front door, stumbled into the house, and slammed the door shut behind me.

Ella leaned over and whispered something inaudible to Jesse, and he nodded. "Poor Leesie. We had all planned to go together, but she told us she'd never be able to get permission," he stated glumly.

After a weighted pause, he shrugged it off and wandered away, and Ella followed.

Phase four: complete. Now, I had nothing to do but wait.

It was dinnertime when it happened. My dad had been cooking that night, and he called us to the table. I got there first, and sat in my usual spot. As my dad brought the soup to the table, he was looking at me in a weird way.

"Hi," I greeted him awkwardly.

"Leesie, I was thinking about what you said last night. About how this is your last chance to tour London and see all the landmarks from the show." My breath caught in my throat. The words I'd been expecting and hoping to hear were finally being spoken, and that excited me.

"Yeah, but I don't have enough money. Ella and Jesse are going, and they were only able to afford it because their parents are paying half."

My dad made some considering noises; he was thinking about it. "How much?"

"1500 dollars," I breathed.

"Hmm," he began. "That's a lot of guacamole."

Before he could come to whatever conclusion he was approaching, my mom stepped into the kitchen, carrying her book. "Hey."

"Hey, Mom," I grumbled in response, maybe a little sadder than I'd intended. She looked at me and sighed, then proceeded to place her book down on the table in a way that screamed, "I'm very concerned and will be shortly delivering some sort of anecdote for your current issues."

"Sarah, I've been-"

"Nat, I was-" my parents began talking simultaneously. They both stared at each other, silently deciding who would speak first.

My mother won. "I've been thinking that maybe we should give Leesie a sort of... last hurrah," she started. I almost jumped up and down in my seat. My dad gave back an extremely confused look. "Her friends are going on some sort of Europe trip, and they said they'd love to have her go with," my mom explained, twisting the exact words of my friends only a little.

My dad looked as if he'd just seen a door open by itself. "But... I was about to say we should let Leesie go to London, to fulfill her childhood dreams."

My mom's look of bewilderment made butterflies erupt in my stomach. "Wait, was she talking to you about that?" I felt the sudden urge to run out of the room, partially due to an impending explosion of laughter and partially because I didn't want to go through an interrogation session.

"No, I was the one who brought it up," my dad assured her. I exhaled and relaxed. "You know, all the locations from Leesie's favorite episodes of *Doctor Who* are there."

The exasperated look on my mother's face was priceless; she heard about *Doctor Who* far more than she would've liked. "Ah, yes, that show you two love so much." She rolled her eyes. "We'll talk more about the trip after dinner." I took that to mean, "We'll talk more about the trip when Leesie's not around."

The next few minutes were filled with nothing but the sounds of spoons and slopping soup. It was delicious, but eerily silent. Europe was on my mind, but I didn't dare mention it. Finally, my father started spewing about his work day, which at least put some sound waves into the dense air.

As soon as I was finished, I ran upstairs to my room, to let my parents have their discussion. I pressed my ear up against my door to try and hear what they were saying, but I couldn't. The only thing I could be sure of was that they were, in fact, talking.

I was violently texting both Jesse and Ella, trying to distract myself and wait patiently for my parents to finish talking. It was at least three days later when my parents called me down again. I texted, "Here goes nothing," to both of them, and tried to prepare mentally for either the best or the worst.

A voice came over the loudspeaker. "Now pre-boarding flight 1623 servicing John F. Kennedy airport in New York. Those who need assistance, families with young children, and anyone requiring extra time may now board."

"Ooh!" Ella squeaked. "It's not much longer!"

"Mm, hmm." Jesse nodded in agreement, though he looked completely oblivious to what Ella was saying; he was absorbed in his lacrosse magazine.

"I better go to the bathroom before we board." Ella stood up, peering around.

"Mm, hmm," Jesse replied again.

Without taking any notice of him, Ella spotted a bathroom and trotted away.

A few minutes of silence passed, then Jesse abruptly threw his magazine to the ground. "John Grant is retiring!" he yelled loudly. People's heads turned in our direction. I nodded unsurely, patting Jesse on the back.

"I don't know what to do with my life anymore. Johnny's gone soon, and we're almost finished with the bucket list. What am I going to spend my time on afterward?"

I laughed a little. "Jesse, we're halfway done with the list. At most. And anyway, you could always play lacrosse instead of watching someone else."

Jesse turned towards me. "But John is awesome. His awesomeness rivals all other awesomeness. And half is a lot. All that's left besides this trip is the MOA, and writing and singing a song."

"I still need to find my perfect dress, and that could take years," I told him, but in my mind, I too was realizing how little we had left. "And zip-lining, that too!" I added. "Those things will keep us busy for the rest of the summer; we only have a month left." I had meant to provide consolation, but Jesse's face fell.

Just then, Ella came back, and the conversation dwindled out. Both Jesse and I were left to marinate in the realization that we were around the corner from the end.

We finally got on the plane, and I was in the window seat. For the first half hour of our flight, the three of us played Jesse's portable little Apples to Apples set. After exhausting that, we were left to our own devices. I rested my head on the window and watched the world shrink below me, until the noise of the whirling engines lulled me to sleep.

"Leesie, don't be startled, but we sort of crashed," Jesse whispered into my ear. "No, no, no, don't freak out. It's okay. We're going to find our way out of the jungle and be alright."

My eyes sprang open and I launched up, the seat belt tugging me back down and causing even more shock.

"Is everything alright, ma'am?" the flight attendant asked me.

"Uh, yeah, sorry," I stuttered.

She stared at me for a moment more before speaking. "Okay... The plane will be landing shortly."

I nodded as I slowly regressed into my chair.

I waited until the flight attendant turned her back to swat Jesse's shoulder. "You absolute jerkwad!" I whisper-shouted at him, but his grin remained radiant.

Ella had apparently been asleep as well, because my voice made her lift her head with a groggy expression. "We there yet?" she mumbled. I continued to stare at Jesse, giving him the chance to relish in my anger.

The plane began to descend through the clouds, and I eagerly looked out the window, hoping to catch of glimpse of the famous New York City skyline.

Jesse suddenly shut the shade on the window, causing me to flinch, and said, "Not yet. We can't experience New York until we *officially* visit."

I turned to him and groaned in protest, but he kept holding down the window shade.

"The city so nice they named it twice" was not quite as nice when all you had to go off of was the noisy, crowded airport. By the time our layover ended and we were boarding the next flight, I was ready to ditch the trip and curl up under my covers, scrolling through Tumblr for at least six hours.

Despite my desire to abort the trip, I sat through the long plane ride. When we finally landed in England at 12:30 in the morning, we were ready for some quick food and a good night's sleep.

My eyes were closed and my thoughts were drifting away into dreamland at last, when all of a sudden Jesse dug his elbow into my arm.

"Gah! What now?!" I angrily whispered, sick and tired of being woken up by Jesse.

"Shh. Ella's asleep. I want to tell you about something."

"I was asleep too, you moron."

"Fine," he concluded. "I guess you don't want to hear about it."

I groaned, accepting checkmate. "Ugh. Alright. Tell me then."

He stared at me, looking as if he was pondering my existence. "Well, go on!" I urged.

He sighed, and began, "Well, I was thinking during the plane ride. My magazine got boring after the third reread. And I just... remembered something." It suddenly hit me that Jesse was stone cold serious.

"You remember Molly Andrew's party, way back?" My heart skipped a beat. Had Jesse gone to talk to Taylor as well? "Nevermind, I don't know why you would. Anyway, this chick from school threw a party at her house, and I got invited. Because, well, look at me," Jesse stated, still completely serious. "I didn't stay long, because people were passing around some things... bad things: drugs." My mind was racing now.

He continued, "I think it was Ecstasy. And Tate was there. I asked her if you were there, because... well, I mean... anyway, as I was saying goodbye, I saw one of her friends passing around the stuff." Jesse fell silent.

"No," I asserted. "No. Tate would never do drugs. She's not the type." Her suicide had thrown half the things I thought I knew about her out the window, but I was sure about this.

"That's what I thought too. But I don't know... she became so weird before the suicide."

I nodded. That was true, but I couldn't imagine Tate doing drugs. Not even the war-torn doppelganger she was by the end of her life.

"Anyway, we've got to get some sleep tonight; we have a busy bucket list conquering day tomorrow." Jesse got up and trekked back to his bed.

The near-sleep zone I had been in before Jesse had nudged me wasn't returning, and my mind refused to empty. I couldn't find peace; my thoughts were buzzing with questions about Tate, about Ecstasy, about her depression and suicide. What had she not been telling me? So much. It was as though, in her last days, I stopped being her best friend. Or friend at all, really.

I stayed up for hours, rolling this way and that, trying desperately to let sleep engulf me, but the more I reached for it, the farther away it retreated. This led to me worry that I would be too tired to do anything the next day, and all the hard-earned money I'd spent to get to Europe would be wasted, and I'd never be able to finish the bucket list. And that worry made me more restless, which made me worry even more. It really was a vicious cycle, my thought process. So vicious that it kept me awake until 4:30, when my exhaustion finally overwhelmed my thoughts.

Complimentary breakfast. As if England wasn't already divine enough, our British hotel had everything you could imagine laying out for the plucking. Bacon, eggs, pancakes, toast, french toast, waffles, tea, sausage, muffins, oatmeal, yogurt, cereals of all kinds, croissants, various fruit, and I'd go on but I've said this whole sentence with just one breath and I must stop soon or I'll die.

So, we gorged ourselves, and afterwards, Jesse and Ella were excited to go out and "experience England."

"I'm not feeling that great. You guys should go without me and I'll stay here and rest for a while."

Ella's face fell. "Are you sick?" she asked with concern in her voice.

"No, no," I assured her. "just jet-lagged. And I didn't sleep well last night." I looked over at Jesse, and our eyes locked on each other, just for a moment.

"Oh, okay. When do you want us to come back for you? Before lunch?"

I wasn't about to miss a chance to devour more delicious British cuisine. "Yes, always before lunch."

So the two of them set off to take a bus tour or some other boring activity, and even though I was sad to see them prancing off together like old married unicorns, I was relieved for the opportunity to catch up on some much needed sleep.

I changed back into my pajamas, excited at the prospect of rest, but as soon as I flopped down onto the bed my mind began racing. I should've gone to that party. I could've stopped Tate from taking the drug, if she even did take it. But that wasn't my responsibility; I wasn't her babysitter.

Tate's friends shouldn't have offered drugs to her. They should've warned her what a bad idea they are.

I tried to find other explanations, but none of them made nearly as much sense as Jesse's drug theory. I thought a lot about that pill case I found in Tate's room. Maybe addiction was what started the depression, and everything that happened afterwards simply made things worse.

I wasn't sure what to do with that idea, but I felt obligated to do something. So, I decided to tell Jesse about Taylor, Brad, and the pill case once he got back. He'd know what to think about everything, and what to do.

But that plan was thrown to the wind, when around lunchtime, Jesse threw open the door of the hotel room whilst hollering "Stay With Me" by Sam Smith. Ella trailed behind him, looking much less enthused.

After his dreadful concert came to a close, he turned to me, and said in an awful imitation of a British accent, "Oh, my, God. You will not believe the absolute charm of the local population, Leesie." Jesse tossed his jacket onto the bed, making a victorious sort of grunt-like noise, and explained further. "I just met a beautiful, fiery, saucy," here he paused and wiggled his eyebrows ferociously, "British gentlelady by the name of Clara." He pronounced Clara in such an elegant fashion that I gagged.

Ella flopped down onto our bed next to me as though she had lost all will to live. I imagine she'd been hearing quite a lot about Clara already.

"There I was, strolling down some avenue. A man with a pocket watch passed by, and I said, 'Good day, sir.' You know, just to be neighborly. And then, as I was looking in his direction, I caught the eye of a gorgeous English maiden. I strolled across the street and and said to her, 'Hey, I lost my number. Mind if I borrow yours?' She rolled her eyes of course."

"You did not say that!" I burst out. That was so cheesy. I copied his accent, and asked, "Has the moist air made you ill? Why would you believe you'd stand any chance with that line?"

He dropped the accent. "Wait, it gets better," he assured me. Then he continued in his British voice, "As I was saying, she rolled her eyes in a frankly attractive sort of way, and muttered, 'Stupid Americans...' Honestly, it was an honor to be offended by such a goddess. Anyhow, she proceeded to give me her number. Tonight, I get to see my lovely again; we are going on a date."

"You've already called her?"

"Six times." Jesse smiled in a tranquil way. "By the fifth, she was all for it."

I was pretty horrified by the thought of Jesse calling this poor girl until she finally agreed to go out with him. I glanced at Ella to verify Jesse's claims.

She nodded glumly.

"This is what happens when I'm not around to chaperone you."

"What? If I kiss her tonight, it'll cross one more thing off the bucket list for me. You need to get out and meet some guys too, if you want to have any hope of checking it off."

"I'm working on it!" I shot back at Jesse. He slyly grinned, then changed the subject back to Clara.

I really wanted to talk to Jesse about Tate. However, he was too entranced by his memory of Clara, so I kept my thoughts to myself. I could wait until he was serious again.

"Leesie?" he broke in the middle of a sentence about British girls' hair.

I looked up. "Hmm?" I hadn't been listening, and hoped he wouldn't question me.

"You alright?"

I smiled and scoffed, nodding in an uncertain way. I really wanted to be alright, at least. I also really wanted to be able to flirt with cute British boys, but where did I start? I was not the flirting type. And mostly, I really wanted to be able to talk to Jesse about his drug theory, but he was too enthralled with Clara.

Jesse acknowledged my not-so-convincing response with nothing more than a pat on the shoulder. "Lunch will cure anything you've got. Where should we go?"

Ella suggested, "How about that restaurant I saw a few blocks away?"

"Lovely idea. Ella will take us to her restaurant and Leesie will be cured. Come." Jesse beckoned to us, and after groaning I followed him out the door, not caring that I was still wearing pajamas.

The restaurant was a nice little joint, and we all got to try signature English fish and chips. I don't really know why they're called "fish and *chips*" because any careful observer would be able to see that the aforesaid chips were actually french fries. There were some parts of Great Britain I was never going to understand, but the meal was delicious nonetheless.

After dining, Jesse claimed we needed to go back to the hotel so he could start getting ready for his date, regardless of the fact that it was five hours away.

Once we returned, I finally changed out of my pajamas. I didn't mind the weird looks at first, but they had really gotten on my nerves as our lunch progressed.

And, while we were back at the hotel, I decided to Skype my

mother. She answered in three rings, which I consider pretty impressive. She was on the desktop in our living room.

"Hi Leesie! Is everything alright? Is the hotel okay?" As she greeted me, my dad came in from the kitchen, holding his morning coffee.

"Yeah, Mom. Everything's great. We've been having lots of fun." I left out the tidbit that all I'd done so far was eat and sleep, but that wasn't important.

"Hey, Leese!" My father sounded a bit too enthusiastic; after all, it was only seven in the morning their time. "How's it hanging? When's your tour?" He was referring, of course, to the Dr. Who tour of London.

"It's tomorrow," I answered.

The conversation continued in the usual manner. Once they were assured I was doing well and that we were all safe, we said our goodbyes and hung up.

"Want to go to the park and look for some cute boys?" Ella asked. She was obviously thinking of the object on Tate's list, "Kiss a British guy." I grinned and agreed.

By the time we got to the nice little park near our hotel, I was having second thoughts about trying to creepily entrance a British guy. "You start looking for some game. I'm going to read for a while," I told Ella. She nodded, then cheerfully walked away. I'd never taken Ella as the super-interested-in-boys type, but maybe I was wrong.

I sat on a wooden bench, opened my book, and began reading. Maybe I was just further exhausting my antisocial tendencies, but I didn't care.

However, the universe had some plans of its own, apparently. Right as I was beginning to read, I saw movement out of the corner of my eye. I glanced up as a handsome boy with brown hair and deep chocolatey eyes sat down next to me. And not on the other end of the bench, either, directly beside me. This was my chance.

"Who's your favorite character?" I asked, looking back to my book.

"I beg your pardon?" Oh my, he had a nice voice too; a delicious accent.

"I'm assuming you came over to discuss this book." I gestured to Tate's copy of *Just One Day*. "You must be a diehard fan."

He smiled and chuckled, "No, actually, I've never read it. I came over because I saw a cute girl all alone on a bench. But now I realize she's American, and I can't go off flirting with an American girl."

I opened my mouth, pretending to be offended. "Well, excuse me, but I am much smarter and more sophisticated than the average American."

"Well, you're still talking to me, so I assume that must be true." He smiled again and held out his hand. "Oliver. But you can call me Ollie." I took his hand and shook it.

"Elise. But if you value your life, call me Leesie."

"Two minutes in, and you're already threatening me? This relationship is speeding by."

"It better; I'm only here for two days."

"We don't have much time together then." He dramatically grabbed one of my hands as if losing me would be heartbreaking.

I laughed.

Ollie said, "So, would you care to dine with me tomorrow night?"

I pretended to think about it. "I suppose..." I agreed finally.

"Okay, how about over there, see that restaurant?" He pointed across the park to a quaint little corner building. "They have amazing bread."

Now, if you know me at all you know one thing: I am never going to turn down amazing bread. "That sounds great. When should I meet you there?"

"Six?" he suggested. "If that doesn't get in the way of any of your tourist-y plans."

"Six sounds great." I really wasn't sure what to do or say next. So I looked around the park until I spotted Ella chatting with a blond guy. We locked eyes and Ella did this weird eyebrow wiggle thing. I laughed out loud.

I realized a moment too late how weird it would seem to Ollie. "Um, that's my friend over there," I assured him.

"Hm, looks like she scored big as well." Ollie stood up, smiled, and walked away. I laughed a bit at how randomly he took his leave, then turned back to my book, unable to conceal my smile.

The next day was a busy blur. We visited tons of tourist sites, from Big Ben to the London Eye. But the highlight was the legendary *Doctor Who* tour.

Halfway through, while we were heading to Cardiff to visit the Millennium Centre, Jesse asked me, "Why are you doing this tour? It must be quite boring for you."

"Jesse, I wasn't lying about becoming a Whovian. I may have started watching for leverage, but now I am definitely a fan of the show," I responded.

"Hmm..." Jesse mumbled, obviously not yet convinced. I made a mental note to watch one or two episodes with him sometime.

When we stopped at a Dr. Who speciality shop, I bought my dad an awesome TARDIS mug that I knew he'd love. I had a lot of fun in that store, but we weren't able to stay long; the tour guide wanted to keep moving.

For the majority of the tour, Jesse was babbling about how lovely his date was and how Clara had looked "stunning as the moon." (Is the moon really that stunning?) They were going on another date that very night, apparently because "his Clara" insisted upon it.

Ella and I both had dates that night as well, with our guys from the park. Even though we didn't attach possessive pronouns before their names, we were nearly as excited as Jesse. Ollie seemed really great, but I was nervous about going on a date with someone I had just met.

Nonetheless, I prepped for the date along with the other two, and was the first to head out. I wore Jesse's perfect dress, the pink flowery one from Hollister. As I ambled across the park to the cafe, I stuck my hands deep into the pockets to keep from nervously picking off my rosey-colored nail polish.

When I got there, Ollie hadn't arrived yet, but I didn't mind. It gave me a chance to lean back in my chair and take a few deep breaths. A waitress brought me bread, and it was scrumptious.

A few minutes passed, and Ollie strolled in. "Hey, Leesie," he greeted with a smile.

"Greetings, Oliver."

"I thought I told you: I go by Ollie," he scolded as he sat down.

I shrugged. "But you didn't threaten me."

"Touché." He grinned.

The waitress returned and handed us menus. Ollie sat back in his chair and asked, "So, what brings you to England?"

"Well, I have a bucket list that I'm trying to complete this summer before I go off to college."

"College? You mean, uni?"

I laughed, and rolled my eyes. "Yeah, uni. Anyway, one of the things on the list is 'Kiss a British guy.'"

"Ahh, my eyes have been opened. I see now where your interest in me is rooted. It's alright, though. I'm cool with being used."

"Oh, what? You think I wanted to kiss you?" I questioned, trying to sound serious.

Just then, the waitress came to our table with some tea. Ollie was trying to hide his face of confusion and embarrassment.

After the waitress left, Ollie replied, "Oh, well I was, I mean..."

"Whoa, I don't know if I really feel for you in that way." I was getting a kick out of teasing the poor guy. "We barely know each other. Don't be creepy."

"Yeah, I know. Sorry." His face was flushed.

"Well... I guess maybe it isn't so bad. This might be my only chance, and you're not *that* awful."

Ollie's face suddenly filled with confidence. "Oh, I get it. You're winding me up. Even though you're so rude, I suppose, because I am a good Samaritan, I will help you with your bucket list."

"Oh really?" I flashed him a brilliant smile. "Go on then."

He raised his eyebrows. "Now? Well, alright."

He leaned in across the table and I met his lips in a not-so-brief kiss. Let's put it this way: Ollie was in no rush to get home.

It was me who *finally* decided to pull away, and he smiled back at me once I did. I didn't know what else to do, so I pulled out the list and drew an overexaggerated check next to "Kiss a British guy." "Thanks, that was... uh... nice," I complimented.

"You're very much welcome." He nodded, as though this was just another day at the office for him.

The rest of the date went smoothly, and by the end of it I was feeling absolutely ecstatic. I had to say goodbye to Ollie, which sort of sucked, because he seemed a guy I would have been friends with back home. Right before we parted ways he kissed me once more; to put it in his own words, "As a buy one get one free discount."

☑ Kiss a British guy

☐ GO TO THE TOP OF THE EIFFEL TOWER

"Ring-a-ding-ding. Leese, it's time to board the Paris express," Jesse said, wheeling my suitcase up to my bed.

I sat up, surprisingly awake. "You packed all my stuff?" I asked Jesse, looking at my zipped up suitcase.

"Sure did," he answered, now focused on packing his own clothes.

"Oh," I began. "Well, thank you."

He turned around and shot me a meaningful glance. "You're welcome."

Let's be real; Jesse was never buying my "I'm feeling sick" story from two days before; he knew I was having a rough time. I was starting to realize how instinctively intuitive Jesse was. Maybe I was wrong all those years ago about him being single layered.

I felt strangely melancholy as we left London behind. I was excited to go to Paris, but part of me was heartbroken that I may never visit England again.

The train ride was basically the exact same as a ride on the Hogwarts Express, so I feel no need to explain. Imagine me telling Jesse he had dirt on his nose, while Ella bought tons of candy from the trolley lady. Other than that not much happened during the train ride.

Lulu was already at the station waiting for us when we arrived. "Ella!" she greeted ecstatically, sporting a thick French accent.

"Oh my gosh!" Ella squeaked, then ran up to give Lulu a hug.

"It's been so long! 'Ow 'ave you been?" Lulu asked.

"Amazing! Hey, come meet my friends." Ella dragged Lulu by the arm to where Jesse and I stood. "This is Jesse, and you remember Leesie," Ella introduced.

"Ahh, yes, 'ello!"

The cordial greetings were made, and then we walked a few miles (ugh, physical activity) to Lulu's college.

When we got there, we met her roommate, Staci, who didn't speak much English. Regardless of this, Jesse and Staci seemed to hit it off. I found their friendship incredibly surprising considering all Jesse could say in French was "treehouse," and all Staci could do in English was order beer and say, "I don't speak English."

Lulu soon found herself fully occupied as a translator, so Ella and I laid blankets on the floor to make our trio somewhere reasonably comfortable to sleep.

After setting everything up, we set off for lunch. I had expected to go somewhere to get a glob of something fancy with some sauce drizzled all over it on a snow white plate, but the restaurant we went to was much different from that expectation.

In fact, it was a buffet. It was practically the complimentary breakfast from London, except with lunch and dinner food. This made it an instant hit for me (and Jesse.)

As we began devouring our first helpings, Staci said something to Lulu in French. Lulu laughed. Ella asked, "What did she say?"

"Oh, nozing, nozing," Lulu assured in her thick accent.

"What?" Ella pressed.

Finally, after what felt like *hours* of Ella's begging, Lulu relented. "She said zat you Americans fit your, um..." she hesitated. "I don't know ze word. What people say about you."

"Stereotype?" Jesse suggested.

"Yes, yes, zat."

Ella inquired, "How do we fit it?"

"Well, it's just, you enjoy eating very much."

I might've been offended by this, but Jesse burst out laughing, which made me rethink my reaction. It was pretty funny. Soon all five of us were bent over cracking up, and we started getting weird looks from the other restaurant patrons.

But they couldn't stare at us for long; we had places to go and things to see. After we ate, we rode the subway down to the more touristy part of town.

At first, the ride was completely void of conversation. Jesse broke the silence by casually asking, "So, Ella, play any sports?"

"Yeah, I play softball. How about you?"

"Oh, you're one of those girls?" Jesse said with fake judgement in his voice.

I don't think Ella realized he was joking. "Uh, yeah?"

A long, incredibly awkward silence followed. For a few seconds, it filled the air with its density, then Jesse said, "Nah, softball girls are cool. I used to date one."

"Oh," Ella said quietly. "Cool."

Gosh. They were *so* awkward. They were both emitting an aura of pure discomfort. I was glad they had me around to interject, "Look, guys! We're almost there."

Downtown Paris looked like a post-card picture. Small cafes and park benches lined every street, while the Eiffel Tower loomed prominently in the distance.

We walked aimlessly for a while, then Lulu and Staci guided us to the Arc de Triomphe. It was pretty, but there were so many people around that it felt clogged.

We had chosen a not-so-great time to come, because Bastille Day (the French version of the Fourth of July) was the next day, so tons of people had swarmed to Paris to watch the parade and the fireworks shooting off of the Eiffel Tower.

However, it would give us the perfect opportunity to cuddle

under fireworks, which was on the list. Plus, it was fun! Who wouldn't want an extra holiday?

That evening, we made it back to the dorm room both fulfilled and exhausted. We had tasted some delicious Parisian cuisine, seen some sights, and learned to say a few phrases in French. (All of which I already knew; Yay public school!)

As we prepared to go to sleep, Ella asked me, "Isn't it going to be weird if we sleep next to Jesse?"

I shrugged. "Nah, he's totally gay."

Ella's eyes widened, and she looked at me, trying to decide if I was serious. "Really?" she whispered.

"No..." I responded. "Well, maybe."

"Hmm." Ella proceeded to lie down next to where Jesse had set up his pillow.

Throughout the night, we all talked and laughed and told stories and whatnot. Staci tried to keep up, but eventually fell asleep due to a lack of understanding, and, presumably, boredom.

Once Jesse and Lulu had fallen asleep, Ella and I were the only ones left standing (well, technically lying.) The late-night drunkenness had kicked in, making absolutely everything fair game for conversation.

We'd been comparing our experiences with our British dates and laughing ourselves silly when Ella suddenly changed the subject. "Can I ask you something?"

"Um, sure," I answered curiously.

"Why the rush?"

I was confused by her question, and hesitated before asking, "What?"

"Sorry." Ella backtracked, "I mean, with the bucket list. Why are you trying to finish it before the summer ends?"

"Oh." I thought about it. I wasn't even sure what the answer was. "I guess I want to get it over with. Move on."

"So you're doing all this to help you move on before college?"

"No matter how hard I want to fight it, it has to end there. I can't live in grief anymore. I want to move on with my life."

Ella smile sadly to herself, from what I could see of her in the darkness. "I never quite got the hang of moving on."

"Who'd you lose?" I asked, then added, "If you don't mind my asking."

"Nothing big: a boyfriend here, a goldfish there. My gran when I was little, but I was so young I can hardly remember it. Incomparable to what you've had to go through."

My conversation with Jesse back in California flashed through my mind. I said, "You can't move on without someone. That's as good as running away. To truly move on, you've got to take them with you."

"Wow, that's... true," Ella responded. "Where did you learn to live like that?"

"After accidentally making out with the guy who said it," I answered, looking towards Jesse.

Ella's mouth fell wide open. "Oh my God, are you guys, like, a couple?" she squeal-whispered.

"No, of course not! In his dreams maybe."

"But, do you like him? Like, *like* like him?" Ella raised her eyebrows rapidly.

"No!" I cried, a bit too loudly. Jesse stirred between us in his sleep.

Ella held up her hands defensively. "Okay, okay," she whispered. "But do you think he likes you?"

I sighed. "Let me tell you something about Jesse: he has a mini-crush on every female he's ever met. Do I think it's anything to worry about? No."

We both erupted into a fit of giggles.

When our laughter slowly fizzled out, Ella groaned. "I feel like I'm going to vomit."

"Oh no! Are you sick?" I whispered worriedly.

Ella yawned, and I quickly checked that I was out of the line of fire. "No, just overtired, I think. We should maybe get some sleep."

"Yeah," I agreed. "I hope you feel better in the morning."

"I'm sure I will."

I didn't know what else to say, so I simply murmured, "Goodnight, Ella."

"Goodnight, Leesie," she responded peacefully, as I drifted off to sleep.

The next morning, Ella woke up with a headache and nausea. I felt bad for keeping her up half of the night, and I was wondering if that had contributed to her sickness.

Jesse and I told her she should rest, but she insisted on coming to the top of the Eiffel Tower with us. Some things just can't be missed.

It was July 14th, French Independence Day. It was bound to be a fun day; there would be fireworks shooting off of the Eiffel Tower and a parade through the streets. But there would also be huge crowds.

Lulu and Staci weren't coming with us to the top of the tower, because they wanted to watch the military parade from the ground. I didn't blame them; even the French president would be in it. However, as Americans, we decided an aerial view would suffice, so we headed off into the crowded streets.

On the way, we stopped by a small bustling bakery and ate some crêpes to hold us over until we got onto the tower. According to rumor, there was a fast food place up there with really good waffles. I wasn't going to pass that up.

Once we arrived, we began waiting in the endless line. Or, as the family of British people standing in front of us called it, "the queue." I was thankful for the crêpes we had eaten, but soon the hunger reclaimed me.

We had paid for tickets to the elevator (or, rather, "the lift,") but the line was what really cost. The tickets were reasonably priced, but the wait was unreasonably long.

However, I had come mentally prepared. I had expected the line, as had my companions. We could be patient. Plus, the weather was a perfect seventy-five degrees Fahrenheit. The sun shone as the gentle breeze played with my hair.

When we finally squeezed into the claustrophobic elevator, it only took us to the second floor, two thirds of the way up. If we wanted to go to the top level, we would have to take another lift.

In order to complete the bucket list, we had to go to the top. But, we decided not to get into the new line immediately. First, we could enjoy the views (and cuisine) from the second floor.

It was there that we discovered the famous waffles, and behold! They were even more delicious than legends foretold. We took the Nutella-covered heaven-nuggets to the observation deck and looked out over beautiful Paris.

After we'd finished stuffing our faces, the three of us waited in another long line to go yet higher into the sky. The wait didn't bother us, though.

Ella was still feeling sick, but Jesse and I were doing our best to distract her, and she seemed to be enjoying herself in spite of everything. "It's all so romantic, you know?" she said as we slowly made our way closer to the elevator. "Going to Paris to complete your late best friend's bucket list. It's very storybook-esk."

I nodded. "Tate would've loved it. She was the sentimental one."

"You say that," Ella replied, "but you're the one who stuck around to do all the sentimental stuff."

I smiled. "True."

Jesse interjected, "It's because Leesie's the brave one."

I looked up at him, a bit shocked by the statement. Did Jesse really think of me that way? We locked eyes, and he winked. I scoffed.

By the time we finally got crammed into the "lift," I was seriously doubting if going to the top would be worth it. However, all of my doubts were demolished as soon as I set eyes on the beautiful view.

On one side, we could see the park where we'd be watching the fireworks that night. People were already starting to gather on picnic blankets, saving their places. On the other side, I could see what looked like some sort of government building.

The three of us walked around slowly, taking everything in, but after about ten minutes, Ella told us to go on without her. She leaned against the fence, looking extremely nauseous as Jesse and I walked away unsuradly.

"Poor Ella," I said once she was out of earshot.

"Yeah, she's got rotten luck."

"Oh look!" I pointed. In the distance, I could see the Arc de Triomphe, which we'd visited the day before.

We gazed out at it for a few seconds, then continued our leisurely stroll.

"So, I never asked. How was your date with the British guy?"

I laughed. "It was fine. Yours?"

Jesse thought about it for a few seconds before saying, "It was adequate. Not planning on going on another with her though."

"Well, yeah. You live pretty far apart."

Jesse nodded. "Yeah. It's not even that though. It's more, hmm... I guess you could say I'm a bit hung up on someone else."

I looked out at the horizon so Jesse couldn't see my face. What was that supposed to mean? Tate? That lacrosse girl Emily? Ella? Me?! Someone I didn't even know about? Finally, I spoke. "Is that so?"

"Yeah... Plus, I don't think I'm regal enough for a British girl."

I faked a laugh, and tried not to dwell on what he'd said.

When we reached the spot with my favorite view, I stopped and stood by the railing.

Jesse also stopped. "I have something I've got to do, and you're not going to like it."

"Um..." I stuttered nervously. Just then, Jesse leaned down and kissed me on the cheek. When he pulled away, I found that my mouth was gaping and I couldn't seem to close it.

"You're reacting better this time," he commented casually.

"I want to slap you right now."

"Yeah, but you're just saying that, not actually doing it, so it's an improvement from California."

I didn't say anything, but squinted angrily at him. A person isn't allowed to say mysterious things and then kiss me on top of the Eiffel Tower, like who did he think he was?

Jesse sighed. "Come on, Leese, we're on top of the Eiffel Tower. I had to do it. For Tate."

I nodded. "Oh. Okay." So it was all just for Tate.

☑ Go to the top of the Eiffel Tower

☐ CUDDLE UNDER FIREWORKS

After seeing the sights, Jesse and I dragged a nearly puking Ella back to Lulu's dorm.

We finally convinced her to get some rest, even though she was clearly disappointed. We tried to provide comfort by reminding her that all Jesse and I were doing for the rest of the day was cuddling and having a picnic. It would be kind of weird with a group of three. (Let's be honest, it'd be kind of weird with any number of people, but that's beside the point.)

Once we had made sure Ella was settled in and comfortable, Jesse and I grabbed a blanket and journeyed back outdoors. Despite the fact that it was still early afternoon, we were headed to Champ De Mars, the park where we'd be watching the fireworks. As we had observed from the top of the tower, good spots were going by the minute.

However, we still had time to stop on the way for dinner. We got sandwiches from a dinky run-down deli, nothing special. It wasn't the food that would be making the moment; it was the location. And, I suppose, the person I'd be with.

We also stopped at a bakery to get some macarons, which I insisted on trying before we left France. They looked so delicious.

After leaving the bakery, we made our way to the park. We picked a grassy area that was far enough away that we could see the whole tower, but close enough that we could see it relatively clearly.

Jesse opened up the blanket and allowed it to fall onto the grass. He looked at me, grinned, and said, "Ladies first."

I sighed at his attempt to be chivalrous, then proceeded to have a seat on the blanket, facing the tower. He sat beside me.

The sun hadn't even started to set, and already strangers were crowding in around us, turning our little blanket into a cell with thousands of guards.

After a moment of silence, Jesse asked, "Want a sandwich?"

I took the slab of bread, meat, and mayonnaise that he handed me and nibbled at the crust. I had wanted to save it for later, but there was nothing better to do, and I didn't feel like talking to Jesse. Actually, I didn't feel like doing anything; I was exhausted. I had been up until three the night before, and I had to stay up late again to watch the fireworks. It was only four and they wouldn't start until eleven. "I have an idea," I stated out of the blue.

"What?"

"Let's nap."

Jesse nodded. "I strongly approve of that idea." He lowered himself so he was lying on his back. I lay down next to him.

I could practically hear Jesse's mind racing with indecision on whether he should try and make a move or not. I turned on my side so I was facing away from him; I didn't want him getting his hopes up. No cuddling would be necessary until the fireworks commenced.

I soon entered a state of half-thinking and half-dreaming. The breeze flitting over my face and the smell of the grass was rather calming, and the sound of people chatting in the distance was like the sound of waves beating against a shore. I was eventually lulled me into a deep slumber.

By the time I woke up, I'd lost all sense of time. I frantically propped myself up on my elbows and squinted at the Eiffel Tower, making sure there weren't any fireworks going off yet. There weren't, meaning I hadn't missed the show. And judging by the sun, I still had quite a while to wait.

Once the panic subsided, I turned to see Jesse talking to a slightly overweight, middle aged guy set up next to us on a blue striped blanket.

"Leesie, you're up! I made a new friend." Jesse grabbed my shoulder and pulled me up into a sitting position.

"Oh um, hello there," I stuttered out groggily.

"Leesie, he barely speaks any English," Jesse scolded. "He can't understand what you're saying."

"Oh," I said, not quite processing the information. Then, when I understood, I burst out, "Wait, how have you been talking to him?"

"He finds my sense of humor absolutely killer. Watch. Hey Julian, *bonjour, maison de l'arbre.*" At Jesse's very clever joke the man erupted into laughter, and Jesse followed. "See, this guy digs me!"

I shook my head. "How do you even know his name is Julian?"

"We had some intense Pocahontas and John Smith communication going on earlier." Jesse nodded as if it was something he did every day.

"Oh." I smiled unsurely. "Okay." I picked up my sandwich so I wouldn't have to talk anymore, and took a miniscule bite. The bread was at least a week old and there was about a gallon of mayonnaise on it. "What time is it?"

Jesse checked his watch. "It's 5:46. You were sleeping for a while."

I nodded, but I was thinking more about the time that still had to pass rather than the time that had already passed. However, I was glad that we had arrived when we did, because I couldn't imagine trying to find a spot in the crowd.

Around six, music started playing through loudspeakers mounted on light posts. The pick-me-up was nice, but half of the music was in French and the other half was entirely composed of Madonna and Bob Dylan. A curious mix.

The sun shone directly into my eyes, until I eventually gave up and turned my back to the tower. All around me, people were laughing and eating and dancing and drinking. There was a feeling of excitement in the air.

I overheard Jesse trying to communicate with Julian again. "Do you live here?" Jesse asked, pointing to Julian and then to the ground. Julian looked bewildered.

"Habitez-vous ici?" I translated.

Julian started speaking wicked-fast French to me. I nodded, trying my best to follow along. When he was finished, I turned to Jesse. "He moved here last year," I told him. "At least, I think that's what he said."

Jesse turned to Julian, nodded, and smiled. "Cool, dude." Jesse held out his fist and Julian bumped it with his own.

From then on, Julian wasn't too focused on us; he was more interested in the friends he'd come with. (One of whom he totally had a crush on, just saying.)

After eating half of my disgusting sandwich, I gave up and handed the rest of it to Jesse. "Here, you can have this."

"Picky picky little Leesie," he teased in a sing-song voice, taking the sandwich.

I punched him on the arm. "Oh please, like you enjoyed yours."

"Leese, it was delicious. And I'm sure this one will be too." Jesse took a gigantic bite as I watched him suspiciously. "Mmm," he said after a few moments. He closed his eyes, and whispered, "Scrumptious."

I couldn't help but laugh at that.

Within half a minute, Jesse had scarfed down the rest of the sandwich.

"It was great," he lectured me once he'd finished. "You're just too picky."

"Not too picky in the guys I hang out with," I responded slyly.

Jesse dramatically placed his hand over his heart. "Ooh, that stings."

I giggled and took one of the pastel pink macarons. "Should we eat these now?"

Jesse shrugged. "Sure. They seem a bit girly for me though."

I tilted my head disapprovingly. "They seem a bit too delicious for you."

"Only one way to find out." With that, Jesse picked up the other macaron and took a tiny bite. He closed his eyes again. "Yum!" he murmured.

"Told you they'd be too delicious for you."

Jesse shrugged it off.

I smile and finally took a small bite. The best way to describe the taste is basically that heaven exploded in my mouth. I fell over onto the blanket. I could hear angels singing opera in the distance. Or maybe that was just more Madonna...

Around us, people gradually grew more enthusiastic as time passed. Slowly the sky darkened, and a star or two sparkled above us. The music pulsed louder and louder, until it finally died down.

I wasn't sure what was happening, and became even more bewildered when the crowd started cheering. "What is happening?" I shouted across the din to Jesse.

"The fireworks are going to start!" he shouted back.

"Oh," I said to myself.

"Yay, we get to cuddle now!" Jesse shouted overenthusiastically.

I blushed profusely, then scooted over and reluctantly let Jesse put his arm around me.

The music started up again, and with it an amazing show. Along with the fireworks, there were also performers climbing the tower and dancing. Moreover, everything was timed to music, which gave it all a fantastical feel of sophistication.

As the minutes passed, I could feel the exhaustion pouring over me, but I was reluctant to close my eyes. I didn't want to miss even a second of the magical show. I did, however, let myself rest my head on Jesse's shoulder, purely for energy reasons, of course. There was simply no other surface that I could comfortably rest on without lying down and giving in to the drowsiness. It's just science.

And well, when Jesse decided to lie down himself, I ended up with my head on his chest due to nothing more than the gravitational pull of the earth. And I had to move my arm around his neck, because its circulation was cut off. And I let myself curl up into him because... well... okay, he was quite comfortable. That's all. Plus, I needed warmth. What else could I have done on a cold night in Paris? Would you have me, a poor young girl, freezing to death just to avoid some intimacy?

Right around when they were releasing a bunch of red and blue fireworks, Jesse kissed my forehead, sort of like he did with my cheek earlier that day. I let it slide again, but then immediately thought to myself, *The first time it's an event. But after the second time, it's expected.* This sent me into a panic, and I acted fast, if not frantically.

"Hey Jess?"

"Yeah?"

"What do you think about Ella?" The question obviously caught him off guard, and I could feel a bit of tension form in his arms, which happened to be wrapped around me.

"Oh, she's pretty chill. We like a lot of the same bands, apparently," he stated. I rolled my eyes at his use of the word "chill." "Why do you ask?"

"Oh, no reason," I lied. Well, thanks to my own quick wit, I had effectively made the situation awkward, Jesse confused, and me slightly jealous. Emphasis on the slightly.

The awkwardness did luckily—I mean, unfortunately—dissipate and we went back to focusing on the night's events.

☑ Cuddle under fireworks

☐ GO SHOPPING IN NEW YORK

"Goodbye, Europe," Ella whispered wistfully as the ground slowly shrunk below us.

Goodbye, consciousness, I mentally mimicked, as I closed my eyes and drifted into a deep slumber.

When I woke up, I found Jesse and Ella absorbed in a deep conversation next to me. I didn't want to participate, so I just looked out the window at the ocean below.

Suddenly, I could see land. "Guys, guys, look!" I punched Jesse's arm repeatedly until he turned to look.

"Land ho."

Squinting, I could make out the famous New York City skyline. The Statue of Liberty loomed evergreen below us, and rising high in the distance was the Empire State Building.

I'm not a huge city lover. Tate was though, and just for a second, I let myself see New York through her eyes. I gaped in awe at the magnificent metropolis that unfurled below me. I felt a strange, gleeful, hopeful fascination. I bet that's what Tate would've felt if she were in my place. And it was spectacular.

When we left the airport, we got into a long line of people waiting for cabs. I'd never ridden in a taxi before, and honestly I was somewhat anxious about it. What if the driver was secretly a kidnapper? "He's going to kill us," I whispered to Ella as Jesse got into the back of a taxi with an angry-looking driver.

"Don't worry; we'll be okay," Ella assured me as she got in.

After a few seconds, I finally worked up the nerve to squeeze in next to her.

"Where to?" the driver asked.

"Fifth Avenue," Jesse responded. Apparently, that was the place to be if you wanted to do some serious shopping.

Despite it being only three o'clock, the streets and sidewalks were packed with traffic. We eventually decided it would be faster to walk, so the driver dropped us off a few blocks away. Turns out he was a really nice guy, and not a murderous kidnapper. Phew.

After several squashed minutes, we pushed through the crowds and emerged onto Fifth Avenue.

Glancing around, I saw more stores than we could possibly visit during our limited timeframe. We had about two hours to shop then we'd eat dinner and head back to the airport. Our flight left at nine.

And so, our epic shopping adventure began. None of us were huge shoppers, but we did all find stores to get excited about. My favorite was the Hershey's store, where I bought my mom a giant chocolate Kiss.

My least favorite? Hollister. When we saw it we had to go in, simply because Hollister was our home terrain and we were in a place so entirely foreign.

We didn't stay there long, because we had new and improved stores to explore.

H&M, the fourth clothing store we shopped in, had an amazing dress that I couldn't stop staring at. It was sky blue with lace, which really doesn't sound like my thing, but it was gorgeous. As I stood captivated, Ella asked, "Do you want to try that on?"

I nodded, grabbed the dress in my size, and bolted to the dressing rooms. Then I had to wait in line. Blah. But when I finally got the dress on, it was even prettier than it was on the manikin.

"I've found it," I said very seriously to Jesse when I walked out.

The best part was that it only cost twenty-two dollars, which is really good for a New York price.

After that, we moved on to my favorite part of every evening: dinner. We ended up at a small joint called "Giolli's Deli and Pizza." The food was mediocre, but let's be honest: all pizza is good pizza, so we considered it a successful meal.

Then it was time we headed back to the airport. So, with a bit of difficulty, Jesse hailed a taxi (apparently it had always been a dream of his) and we told the driver where to go.

The final stretch home was a unique experience, because we were seated in first class. For the first time in forever, I was able to stretch out my legs whilst soaring through the air in a large metal cylinder. So that was fun.

The flight attendant also offered us some snacks aside from the usual peanuts, pretzels or cookies. I took an apple. But that was about where the benefits ended. We still weren't allowed to use electronics during take off, we still couldn't drink alcohol, and we still had to be sitting when we were supposed to be sitting. All reasonable constrictions, but nonetheless disappointing.

I wasn't too devastated though, I was mostly thankful for the peace and quiet. It had been almost twenty hours since I'd last slept, and my eyelids wouldn't stop drooping. Despite wanting to enjoy my first class experience, I finally gave in to the exhaustion and let myself fall asleep.

I was stuck, alone, at Ella's crappy party. I had tried to avoid being dragged along, but Tate insisted that I go.

Now, I sat on some popular girl's uncomfortable leather couch. Tate was off chatting with her school friends, and I didn't have the energy to try to socialize with them.

Suddenly, a boy sat down next to me. "Not a fan of parties, Leese?" Jesse asked.

I just sighed.

"Yeah, me neither. I only showed up because..." he didn't finish his sentence. Then, he gently placed his hand on mine.

Even though his hand was warm and calming, there was suddenly a gnawing feeling in my gut that told me that something was wrong.

I looked at him, and he tilted his head. "Are you okay?" he wondered innocently.

"I need to go find Tate," I blurted, standing up.

"Leesie, you should stay," Jesse said as he stood up too. His voice was so longing, filled with sadness and angst.

"I... I can't, Jesse..." I said, pushing away from him.

I turned and pushed through the dense crowd. I wanted to find Tate. I needed to talk to her about something, something so important that it couldn't wait another second.

I opened a heavy door and made my way down a dark hallway, my steps echoing off the stone floor and walls. I opened a door on the right and peeked in, but it was dark. Tate wouldn't be in there, so I kept walking. Once I had almost reached the end of the hall, I picked another door, this time on the left.

The sun shone in my face and nearly blinded me. Once my eyes adjusted, I saw a figure a few yards away, so I stepped out onto what appeared to be the roof of a very large building.

Going up to the figure, I saw that it was Tate. She was standing near the edge of the roof, and I took a second to check out our surroundings.

We appeared to be standing on top of the Eiffel Tower, only we weren't in Paris, we were in New York. And the high fences that were normally around the decks weren't there. I could look straight down and see taxis and people strolling down the sidewalk. I instinctively took a step back, but Tate stayed there, looking down.

For what felt like too long she was silent. Then she said, "Pretty, isn't it?"

"What?"

"The ideas," she responded calmly. "The idea that this building can make you fall in love. The idea that a city can make your dreams come true."

"I suppose..."

"What about the idea that I could just..." Tate inhaled deeply, "end it. Do you think that's pretty?"

"What?" I stammered again.

For the first time, she looked up at me. She smiled. A breeze blew and I wanted to reach out, make sure she didn't lose her balance. But for some reason, I couldn't. "Tate," I whispered, and felt a burning a my throat. A panic rose in me but I couldn't move.

She looked back down. "It is pretty," she said quietly, almost in a whisper. "It's beautiful." And before I could say anything, she stepped. She stepped and she fell.

"Tate!" I screamed, as my knees buckled under me. "Tate!"

- [x] Go shopping in New York
- [x] Fly first class
- [x] Find my perfect dress

☐ GO ZIPLINING

"Leesie?" Jesse's voice cut through the darkness. "Are you okay?"

I tried to say yes, but I couldn't speak through the sobs. Finally, I choked, "She jumped."

I'm not sure if Jesse knew what was going on, or if he simply saw me there, completely hysterical, and decided that he didn't need to understand. He put his arm around me, and I fell into him. We sat like that, with me crying into his shoulder, until his shirt was wet from tears and I was able to calm down.

"It was a just a dream," I whispered finally. "A stupid dream."

Jesse nodded and then tucked a piece of hair that had fallen into my face behind my ear.

"Thanks," I said, not just referring to the hair.

"You okay now?" he asked gently.

I nodded as a voice came over the speakers, "Ladies and gentlemen, we will be landing in Chicago in about twenty minutes. Please disable all electronic devices, make sure your seat belts are fastened and your tray tables are in the upright and locked positions."

I looked over at Ella, who was sleeping sprawled out over her table. "We should probably wake her up."

At the airport, my parents were elated to see me. And I'll admit, it was nice to see them again too. But seriously, did they have to act like

I had been revived from the dead? My mom was teary-eyed at my return, and my dad hugged me multiple times before we could get to the car. I had to wonder what it would be like coming home from college, when I would've been gone for months, instead of less than two weeks.

As we drove home, Jesse, Ella, and I were rapid-firing off cool things from the trip, while my parents listened intently, possibly for anything that sounded suspicious.

We dropped Ella off at her house, and Jesse at his shortly after. That was the last time I heard from either of them for a while.

For the next week or so, I was very busy between practicing on my little keyboard, working, and moping around. Maybe Jesse and Ella were too, and that was why they hadn't bothered to contact me since the trip.

Now, I don't want to play the victim here. I could've easily called or texted them, and I didn't, but I still thought it was a bit weird that they dropped off of the face of the earth for a week. Finally, I decided enough was enough and dialed Ella.

When she picked up, I could hear the smile in her voice. "Hey, Leese. I was starting to wonder what happened to you."

I laughed. Since when did she call me Leese? Probably from spending so much time with Jesse in Europe. "Yeah, I was getting worried about you too. I was also wondering if you wanted to sleepover tonight."

"Oh that sounds fun! And no need to be worried, I'm not dead or anything," she joked, but almost immediately caught herself. "I mean... uh... Just let me go ask my mom about the sleepover."

"Okay," I said in the most forgiving way I could muster. It's not like the simple mention of death was going to break my heart or something.

That night, as the end credits of an incredibly sappy chick flick played, Ella asked, "So, have you talked to Jesse since Europe?"

"No. Well, I saw him once at work, but we only said hi, we

didn't actually get to talk."

Ella's eyes widened. "Wait, so you're saying you don't know?" She looked as if she could barely contain her excitement.

"Know what?" I demanded, worried about Jesse.

"Well..." She paused. "Don't freak out, okay? A few days ago, Jesse and I went on a date."

"No way," I stated in disbelief.

"Yeah. It was really nice. You're not mad, are you? Because you said you didn't like him, but then I was thinking, maybe you just said that..."

"No, no," I assured her, trying also to assure myself. "Of course I'm not mad. For Pete's sake, I practically gave my blessing. Where did you go?" The question I really wanted answered was why Jesse hadn't told me. It's not that hard to text and say, "Yo, I'm going out with your friend. What should I wear?" Maybe he'd purposefully been ignoring me, because he thought I'd be mad. But, I mean, I had no right to be mad; I wasn't in charge of them.

"We went to this really nice restaurant, with classical music and waiters in suits."

"You did not."

"We did?" she responded hesitantly.

I laughed, unable to hold it in any longer. "Was the name some French version of like the Elegant Salad or something?"

"Yeah, *La Salle Élégante*. Why do you know that?"

I smiled. "Ella, let me tell you a story." And so it happened: I told Ella about my date with Jesse. Everything, from the flowers at the door, to the dancing in the driveway. She was a good audience, laughing at the funny parts and looking all mushy at the romantic ones.

"Oh, Leesie," she sighed when I finished. "I don't know how you could possibly not like him."

"I grew up with him; he's like a brother to me. But you didn't." I did the weird quick-eyebrow-raise-repeatedly-thing and she laughed.

"So are you going out again?!"

"Yeah..." Ella said. "In a few days. But you shouldn't tell him I told you, he might think I'm over eager."

"Of course I won't. Anyway, I've decided you two must now refer to me as Master Third Wheel whenever I am in your presence, do you understand?"

"Yes, Master Third Wheel," Ella chanted as though brainwashed. Then in a concerned tone, she added, "Are you sure you aren't mad? Or sad?"

"Ella," I said, trying to sound both as firm and as confident as possible. "I'm fine. I've dealt with a lot worse than this."

The next afternoon, Jesse and I had work together. "Hey, Leese," he greeted me casually. Maybe the whole ignoring me thing had been in my head. Probably.

"Hi, Jesse." I wanted to bring up Ella, but I didn't want Jesse to think she was obsessed with him.

Jesse leaned against the counter, waiting for a customer to come strolling in. Considering it was two o'clock on a Monday, not many people were shopping. "So, how are things? We've barely talked since we were on the airplane," Jesse said.

I blushed, remembering my embarrassing breakdown on the plane. Ugh, that dream had been awful. "I'm fine. Anything new with you?" I asked, with maybe just a hint of implication.

"I, uh... nothing really."

I waited, nodding slightly.

"Well, there is one thing," he admitted finally.

I nodded again, still remaining silent.

"Ella and I... we..." I cocked my head, waiting patiently for him to spit it out. But before he managed to, a tall muscular guy and his stick-thin blond girlfriend came in to the store. I was so distracted by the girl's worshipping expression that I almost didn't realize I knew her boyfriend.

After we had both stared at each other in stunned silence for a few moments, Brad said quietly, "Hi, Leesie."

Back when Tate had been dating him, the three of us hung out one time. It was pretty much the second-worst experience of my life. Imagine Brad, the big shot football player, and me, the big-shot-football-player-hater, hanging out only because Tate wanted us to.

The two hours consisted primarily of Tate chattering while Brad and I barely uttered a response, until Brad made some lame excuse to go home.

After he left, I questioned Tate, "Why do you even like him?"

She plopped down on her bed. "Leesie, he was just being awkward. He's not usually like that."

I rolled my eyes, and sat in her desk chair. "Oh please. We both know you're only dating him because of popularity."

Looking back on that, I regret it. I really do, but at the time, it felt good to finally put it out in the open. "That's not true!" Tate insisted. "He's funny and caring."

I scoffed. "He's not even that hot."

Tate looked down. "He's my boyfriend, Leesie," she whispered finally. "Why can't you support me?" When she looked up, her eyes were filled with tears.

"I'm sorry," I apologized, getting up, walking over, and sitting next to her on her bed. "It's just... I know you could do better. But I don't even know him. He might be the best guy in the world."

She leaned her head on my shoulder, and we sat there for a long time, with music playing in the background. That was before everything.

So that day at Hollister, I wasn't sure how to feel about Brad strolling in. About him remembering my name. "Hi, Leesie," he'd said, but my tongue seemed incapable of forming words to respond.

In the silence, I looked from Brad to Jesse, unsure of what to do. Finally, I turned and walked away into the back room. I could hear Jesse describing something to Brad; it could've been yoga pants or how my personality isn't usually like this. I didn't care, because I wanted nothing to do with Brad Shager.

While I was loitering in the back, I got bored and ended up reaching for the list in my pocket. I read through everything, and looked back on all that we had accomplished.

In only a few months I had changed so completely I was almost unrecognizable. The worst part was wondering if, when this all ended, I would go back to the braindead, lonely, dispirited Leesie that Tate had created. Moving on still seemed inconceivable.

With a sigh, I folded the list back up, and returned to the checkout counter. "Is Shager gone?" I asked Jesse.

"Yeah," he answered. "Why did you avoid him like that? The poor guy got really confused."

"You know why, Jesse."

"I don't, actually. Why don't you tell me what's up with you, Leesie? You seem off."

"Just forget it," I shrugged. "I'm going home early. Tell Rita I used one of my sick days." Jesse stared questioningly at me for a moment, then nodded and said goodbye hopelessly.

A couple of nights later, I was looking through Jesse's plans concerning our trip to the Mall of America. They were kind of nonsensical, having us waking up at four in the morning and leaving at ten at night to maximize our time spent shopping. As I was reviewing them I heard three heavy raps on the door.

I got up and speed-walked downstairs, expecting Jesse to be there with some sort of urgent news. On my way down the stairs, I heard three louder knocks (more like banging) coming from the other side of the door.

"I'm coming!" I yelled, slightly annoyed. When I opened the door, Jesse was nowhere to be seen. Instead, there were two heavily armed police officers. Without saying a word, they marched into my house.

I would've yelled for my parents, but they were out on a date. I was alone.

The officers began digging through all of our belongings, flinging open drawers and cabinets. "Hey, what's going on?" I weakly, then gathered a little more courage. "What the heck are you doing?" I demanded, shouting over the noise of them tearing my house apart.

One of the cops turned to face me. "Your identity was linked in a case involving the possible usage of illegal substances."

"What?" I asked, appalled. "Do you mean Tate?"

"You have the right to remain silent during this warranted search." That shut me up.

Next, the officers went upstairs. Naturally, I followed them. *Okay*, I thought, *this can*not *be legal.* "You don't have my permission to do this," I told them as they dug through my room.

They ignored me.

One of them picked up the bucket list, which had been laying on my table. "Miss, this is a piece of evidence from the case. Where did you obtain this?" I opened my mouth to speak, but couldn't muster anything in response.

After around thirty seconds of silence, the officer gently placed the bucket list into a plastic bag.

"Hey, no, you can't take that. That's my property!" I yelled, finally finding my voice.

"Please step away, Ms. Derell, or we will be forced to incarcerate you for questioning."

"You can't take my stuff! This is ridiculous," I insisted.

"When and where did you obtain this evidence?" he demanded.

I once again found myself at a deficit for words. "Let's take her to the station. She might know a thing or two."

The other one spoke, gentler. "Miss, if you'll come with us willingly, you won't be cuffed."

Being legally an adult sucked. I didn't respond to that either, but knew I had no choice. I followed them out of my front door and into the police car. My parents were going to freak.

Now, you may remember my previous excursion to the police station. It was about a week after Tate's suicide, and I had barely been able to think, let alone speak, about her. The investigator, Detective White-Guy Harlem or whatever, ended up getting the pleasure of meeting me again.

"Hello, Elise," he greeted me. "It's a pleasure to see you again."

"And you," I replied as sarcastically as I possibly could.

"I am still the investigator on the case, and I would like to ask you a few more questions."

I nodded, but I wasn't thinking about what he was saying. I was thinking about how my parents would react when they came home to the house all torn apart and me gone.

"Did Tate ever offer you illegal drugs?" he read from a list.

"No."

"Did she ever take illegal drugs in your presence?"

"No."

"Were you ever suspicious that Tate had taken drugs?"

"No."

"Honestly, Elise, we can do this the easy way, or the hard way."

"If Tate did drugs, I never knew about it. Like I said last time, we didn't spend much time together in the last few months."

"That doesn't explain why you had a potentially vital piece of evidence in your possession."

"The bucket list?" I asked, incredulous. "You've got to be kidding me. That's nothing more than a childhood memory. It's not a piece of evidence."

"I don't kid, Elise."

A few seconds of silence passed.

"Didn't you search Tate's room?"

"I'll be asking the questions."

"Oh my gosh." This guy was useless. "Then ask something of value."

Harlem was a little taken aback by that, but frankly I didn't care. He didn't scare me or anything. I just wanted to leave.

I elaborated, "If you did search her room, you would've found the bucket list. That's where I got it, when her mother invited me over to get anything sentimental that I wanted."

"Okay, well..." Harlem faltered. "Stay here at the station for a while, while we process your withheld evidence. If it ends up being unimportant, we'll give it back. If we decide you may have had something to do with the use of illegal substance, you'll have more questions to answer. We also need to call the mother to ask if she really did let you take that list. But until then, you can call whoever you want, let your parents know where you are. I'll show you where."

Harlem led me out to a wooden bench, handcuffed me to it, and said, "Now if you need anything, ask Sherri here." He gestured to the plump woman behind the front desk.

"Hey Sherri," I said loudly, so both her and Harlem could hear. "Would you get me a key for these handcuffs?"

Sherri laughed. Harlem looked displeased. Then he said, "If you need to call anyone, use this phone." He gestured to the phone on the wall next to me.

Who should I call? I thought. The only numbers I had memorized were Tate's and my parents, one of whom was dead and the others were on a date that I didn't want to ruin.

"Sherri, do you know where they put my phone?" The officers had taken it from me when I got to the station.

"I've got it right here, dear, but I'm not allowed to give it to you."

"I know," I assured her. "But could you turn it on, go into my contacts and get the number for someone named Jess?"

She looked at me reluctantly, then proceeded to pick up the phone with slight hesitation.

"Thanks," I said. It was perhaps the first non-sarcastic or angry thing I'd said since the police had shown up at my house. "The passcode is 8283."

Sherri read off the number, and I dialled it on the wall phone.

He picked up pretty quickly, and started talking right away. "Okay, so I've been thinking: we don't want to wake up at four in the morning, that's crazy."

I smiled, remembering how comparatively normal my life had been just an hour ago. "That's true. I agree."

"Leesie, are you okay?"

"What?" That's when I realized: I was crying.

"I'm okay... It's just... this really stupid thing happened and my parents are on a date so I need you to come here and get me."

"Okay. Where are you?"

I took a deep breath before answering. "The police station."

Jesse was silent. In the quiet, I could hear both of us breathing.

Finally, I spoke. "These police officers came to my house and they took the bucket list and they got mad that I had it and then they took me here."

"Okay. I'm coming. But I'm calling your parents to let them know."

"No, don't call them!" I insisted, tears springing to my eyes again. "They don't know about the list. They might be mad."

"Leesie," Jesse said in a calming voice, "they won't be mad. I'm on my way, okay? I'll be there in fifteen minutes."

After I hung up, I sat there wringing my hands, worried about how my parents would react to the whole situation. I was thankful Jesse would be the one explaining it to them instead of me.

When he finally arrived, I tried to leap up and hug him, but the handcuff was a bit restrictive. "Whoa," he commented when he saw it. "Is that really necessary?"

"I didn't attack them or anything if that's what you mean," I responded crankily. "But they're not letting me leave until they decide if I stole the bucket list and if I gave Tate drugs."

"It's protocol," Sherri butted in.

Jesse sat down beside me. The wooden bench felt harder and harder the longer I sat on it.

After a minute of quiet, I prodded, "So how'd they take it?"

"They were worried, but I tried to keep them calm. They should be here soon."

"Thanks, Jesse," I said sincerely.

He looked deep into my eyes. "Of course."

After a moment of silence, I asked hopelessly, "Do you think Tate was on drugs?"

Jesse looked around as if checking if anyone was listening. I could tell he didn't think the police station, with Sherri three feet away, was the place to have that conversation. Which explains why he lied. "No." But I could see in his eyes that he didn't mean it.

*Ella sat uncomfortably on the stiff-backed bench, staring at the magazine in her hands.

Suddenly, the glass door swung open. After walking through it, a detective held it open for a distressed woman. Ella realized that the woman was Maddie Conscivit, Tate Conscivit's mother.

Almost immediately, Ella opened her mouth to ask what was wrong, but before she could, the detective guided Mrs. Conscivit toward the back of the police station and into a small office.

Ella tried to return to her magazine, but she couldn't focus; all she could think about was Tate's mom. She was left wondering for a lengthy half an hour, before finally Mrs. Conscivit walked out, looking no better than she had when she'd entered the station.

Ella stood up. "Mrs. Conscivit, what's wrong?" Her instinctive was kindness kicking in. She didn't want to be nosy, but she wanted to help if she could.

Maddie stared at her for a moment, and Ella didn't know how to react. "You're Ella, right?" she said finally.

"Yeah."

For a moment, Maddie looked as though she was going to go into some long speech, but she only said one sentence. "My daughter just killed herself."

Ella was completely shocked. She barely knew Tate, and yet still felt a rush of horror and sadness. Hearing the news, out of the blue, felt like being hit by a train.

Ella dropped her magazine and stated in the most caring voice she could muster, "Oh my God, what happened?"

Maddie didn't respond, and automatically Ella stood up and put a hand on her shoulder. "I'm sorry... I shouldn't ask. That's... awful."

As Maddie began shaking her head, fresh tears spawning in her eyes. "I'll have to tell her..." her voice quavered to the point where it was unrecognizable. She shouted at nothing in particular, "I'm going to have to tell her best friend that she hung herself!"

Without knowing what else to do, Ella looked Maddie right in the eyes.

"I'll tell her," she said softly. Maddie opened her mouth, but before she could move her tongue to speak, Ella repeated, "I'll tell her. You don't have to worry about that. I'll tell her." Ella felt a slight lump in her throat, but no tears.

For what looked to be the first time in years, Tate's mom gave a weak smile. "Thank you," she whispered. "You're a good friend, you know that?"

My mother came into the station with so much fury that I was worried for my life. However, I soon discovered that, thankfully, the fury wasn't directed at me. "I demand to speak to whoever was in charge of this search immediately!" she practically spat at Sherri.

"Yes, ma'am. I'll go get him," Sherri said, slightly flustered. I hate to say I was a little too satisfied with the idea of Harlem getting yelled at by my fuming mother. But I couldn't help blaming myself for their spoiled date.

My dad rushed in right behind my mom, trying to calm her down. "Honey, we're supposed to wait until the lawyer gets here. No harsh actions, remember?" he murmured into her ear after Sherri had left.

Just then, they both caught sight of me. "Leese!" my father said, coming over and hugging me awkwardly, because of the handcuff.

When we pulled apart, he turned to Jesse, and said, "Thank you so much for calling us."

Before Jesse could answer, my dad's focus was back on me. "I'm so sorry this happened. You okay, Leesie-loo?"

Honestly, I felt my dad should be the last one to apologize, but I appreciated the sympathy. I managed to mutter some sort of affirmation that I was okay before my mother cut me off when she saw the handcuff.

"They're treating you like a serial killer. This is ridiculous! And after all you've been through..."

"Mom," I said in the calmest, most comforting voice I could muster, "I'm fine."

"You are everything but fine, Leesie Derell, and I demand there be repercussions for what these so called 'officers' did!"

An exhausted-looking man, who was apparently my lawyer, suddenly came into the police station carrying a small brown briefcase. The three adults conversed in low voices while Jesse and I slumped on the stiff, uncomfortable wooden bench.

After some intense negotiation with Detective Harlem, my handcuff was taken off and I was declared free to go. My mother wasn't dropping the subject that easily, though.

"Your mom is quite valorous towards the local police, I'll give her that," Jesse stated. I chuckled a little and let my head fall on his shoulder.

"Could I stay over at your house tonight?" I quickly added, "Just because my mom's going to be fussing all night long and I won't be able to get any sleep."

Jesse smiled and raised his voice to say, "Mrs. Derell?" My mother turned frantically to look at him. "I'm going to take Leesie back to my house to rest."

"Oh, you're such a darling. Thank you, Jesse," she responded with a smile that dripped with sugary syrup. Of course, she immediately turned back to continue her feud with a now very pale looking, (I mean, even more pale than normal looking,) Detective Harlem.

Jesse mouthed, "Let's go," to me and stood up. I followed him out the door and into his dad's tiny little Prius.

After starting the engine, he turned to me and said, "How about some KFC?"

"How'd you know I needed an endless bucket of chicken?" I responded.

He grinned back. "Kentucky, here we come."

"Seems as if they misheard me; I ordered a fifteen piece, but I got a fifty piece bucket... oh well," Jesse said as he opened up the bag of food while I leaned against the counter.

"Where's Graham?" I asked.

"Probably sleeping already. He's got summer camp every morning at six, and he always goes to bed-"

"I think Tate was on drugs, Jesse." He looked up, right into my eyes. "I think she was on Ecstasy."

He put his arm around my shoulders comfortingly. "I think you might be right, Leesie."

He dropped his arm and grabbed the bucket of chicken, then held it out to me.

"Jesse..." I frowned, not feeling that it was the time for fried chicken.

"Right." He took a piece of chicken out for himself, then put the bucket back on the counter.

"Hmm," I said, realizing for the first time that it almost didn't matter whether or not she was on drugs, because it was too late to do anything about it. After a thoughtful moment, I took a piece of chicken and engulfed it.

"Atta girl," Jesse praised. I rolled my eyes. "You know," he continued, through a mouth full of chicken, "what happened happened. And I wish we could go back and change it, but we can't."

I nodded, grabbed a chicken wing, and took a large bite. I

savored its delicious taste, as Jesse's mom walked into the kitchen.

"Oh," she said upon seeing me. "Hello there, Leesie. Are you spending the night?"

I swallowed my large mouthful of chicken, then responded, "If that's okay."

Mrs. Roe smiled. "Of course. You're always welcome here."

"Thank you."

"Anyway, I'm off to bed. You kids have a good night!"

After the sound of her footsteps had faded, I turned to Jesse. "So, you and Ella, am I right?" I prompted with a sneaky smile on my face.

Jesse sighed. "I'm never going to hear an end to this, am I?"

I laughed. "Nope."

For the next week , I kept busy working, planning, and practicing piano. Because of my "run-in with the law," I had to tell my parents about the bucket list. Even though they wished I'd told them sooner, they weren't mad. They even approved the Mall of America trip, which was good, because I didn't have enough time for another scheme.

As August began, I realized just how close to the end of the summer I truly was. I would be leaving for college in less than four weeks, and that terrified me.

However, I tried to keep my inevitable departure out of my mind, and it wasn't too difficult with everything I had going on. On top of the MOA (Mall of America), I still had five other things to cross off the list, though they weren't as big.

Luckily, I didn't have to figure it out by myself. Jesse and I spent most of our time at work focusing on bucket list scheduling instead of customers. But despite all of our planning, Jesse never failed to surprise me.

One afternoon, I was watching *Doctor Who* in my room, when the doorbell rang. I had gotten into the habit of making my parents answer the door, ever since my encounter with the po-po.

But when I heard Jesse casually chatting with my mother, I figured it was safe to go downstairs. There he stood, with Ella beside him. "Get your shoes on, Leese, and let's go on an adventure."

"Xtreme Thrillz: Skydiving and Fun," Ella read aloud, squinting at the building complex in front of us. "Why are we here? I thought we were going zip-lining..." She sounded genuinely afraid.

Jesse wrapped a reassuring arm around Ella's shoulder, causing me and, I'm sure, every one of you readers, to cringe, and then said, "We are. They don't just do skydiving, they also do family ziplining, family rock climbing, and family canoeing. Which reminds me, you need to get used to using your little girl voice, Leesie, if we want to get that discount for families of three."

"No."

"Aww, come on, Leese."

"I refuse."

Ella laughed. "Oh, it's fine, Jesse. It's only a few dollars."

I remained as silent as possible throughout the next thirty minutes, as we learned how to zip-line and got geared up. It was so weird seeing Jesse and Ella being all cutesy. It made me want to throw up a little, to be honest. They had a sort of pseudo-flirting thing going on, where Jesse would say something, probably completely nonsensical, and she'd giggle. It was bizarre.

So, I found it hard to enjoy myself to the extent I could've during our zip-lining endeavor. I felt the need to keep quiet. Unfortunately, it made the already uncomfortable situation awkward by tenfold.

Ella and Jesse tried their best to make me talk, steering conversations that had nothing to do with me in my direction, but it felt so forced. Besides, it was weird talking to them when they were being so mushy and couple-y. It was like I didn't even know these people.

The highlight of the day was the actual zip-lining, probably to no one's surprise. It felt like I was flying through the forest faster than a jet, but it probably looked like I was going at the speed of an elderly jogger.

About five minutes after the zipline, once the adrenaline had subsided, I again found myself feeling like the awkward third wheel.

Our plans for going out to IHOP afterwards dissolved, and once Jesse had driven me home I was only able to manage a half-hearted, "Bye." I didn't even bother checking off "Go zip-lining" when I got to my room. I could do that later.

☑ Go zip-lining

☐ SHOP AT THE MALL OF AMERICA

The next day, I felt awful. I wasn't physically sick, but I had transformed back into the person I was during the first few weeks after the suicide. I didn't want to eat. I didn't want to move. I didn't want to think.

I called into work and asked Rita if I could have the day off. She easily agreed, and told me she hoped I would get better soon.

I also emailed Ed Perkins, my piano teacher, and told him I wouldn't be able to come to my lesson that night. He was also very understanding.

They pitied me. Even though they didn't know what had happened, they tried to understand. It was nice, but deep inside I hated myself for needing it. It had been nearly three months, and even though I had learned to function with the pain, I hadn't learned to subdue it.

That evening, as I was indulging in my ever-present Netflix addiction, Jesse texted me.

Jess: *You okay?*

Clearly, he was worried because I hadn't been at work. I should've responded with something to calm his nerves, assure him that I was okay, but instead, I changed the subject.

Me: *MOA this weekend?*

Jess: *Yeah. Wanna meet in the treehouse to discuss final details?*
Me: *Sure. Thirty mins, gotta finish my episode.*

When I arrived at the treehouse, Jesse was already there. Squinting at me through the semidarkness, he shouted, "Yes! You brought cheese puffs."

I laughed, and threw the bag up to him, then ascended the ladder.

Concern painted Jesse's face as he asked, "So why weren't you at work?"

"I wasn't feeling the best. Decided I'd sleep in."

"Ahh." An understanding smile spread across his lips. "Playing hooky, I see."

I rolled my eyes. "It wasn't like that."

"Good, because we're going to need all of the money we can get for the Mall."

And so we launched into planning. All that was left unchecked on the list was shopping at the Mall of America, writing a song, getting our cartilages pierced, learning to play piano, and singing in front of a crowd.

"Do I have to get the piercing?" I whined, rubbing my ear.

"If you do it, I'll do it."

"Alright then." Having a needle through my ear would totally be worth it.

The next Friday afternoon Jesse and I found ourselves excitedly pulling out of my driveway, as my parents waved through the living room window.

"Ahh, this feels familiar." I leaned back in my chair while reminiscing about the California trip.

The drive to Minnesota, however, was much more reasonable; it would only take us around seven hours. We had a lot to accomplish during that time, though.

The plan was that we would write a song during the drive,

knocking one more thing off of the list. I was poised and ready with a piano app opened on my phone, so I could play the chords. But first, we had to come up with an idea on what the song should be about.

"Well, it should be about Tate," Jesse suggested. "Since it's for her bucket list. Or we could write it from her point of view."

The ideas were good, but they both sounded horribly unappealing. I wasn't too into reliving my tragic past, I suppose. "Let's write it about her. Less confusing that way."

"Alright, well, then let's start hittin' some chords."

In the end, the song was about Tate and how we felt about her. Letting myself think about her was hard, but writing the song was kind of therapeutic. It was as close as I'd ever come to speaking to her again.

By the time we arrived late at night, we'd spent hours writing the song, and were happy with the final result.

We checked into our dinky hotel a few miles away from the mall. As soon as we dumped our suitcases onto the floor, we both fell onto our separate beds. I managed to set an alarm on my phone and mumble out a goodnight to Jesse. Then, I was asleep.

The next morning, when my phone's alarm sounded, I opened my eyes groggily. Peering around the room, I suddenly remembered where I was. I threw a pillow at Jesse. "Wake up," I commanded. "We have shopping to do."

"So we do," Jesse remarked as he lept out of bed, surprisingly spry for someone who had just woken up. "I'm going to take a shower. I'll be out in ten."

And with that, he ran off to the bathroom with a bundle of clean clothes in his hands. I picked up some of my own clean clothes and got dressed, then threw my slightly greasy dirty-blond hair into a ponytail, too lazy to shower.

After Jesse emerged a few minutes later, dressed in what I suppose he would call mall clothes, we were ready to depart.

The Mall was exceptional. Walking in, we were surrounded by

more stores than I'd ever seen. "Tate would've loved this..." I breathed as we gazed around at all of the shops surrounding us.

"I think anybody would love this," Jesse said, attempting to keep the conversation light.

"Anyone who likes shopping, at least," I agreed. "Where to first?"

We hopped around into a few stores we had never heard of, and bought some small Minnesota souvenirs to bring back to our families.

As we were strolling past Claire's, I suddenly remembered. "Come on, Jesse. It's time," I said while forcibly dragging him into the store.

"But, Leesie," he protested, "this is a girls' store!"

"You said you'd get your ear pierced if I did," I reminded him in a sing-song voice.

"Oh, yeah. You go first then."

So I did. I told the employee, a girl who was not much older than I was, where I wanted it pierced, picked out a stud, and then sat in the chair. Even though I'd had my ears pierced before, I was nervous. I had heard that the upper ear was more painful than the earlobe.

I braced myself, and it was over quickly. I'll admit, it didn't sting nearly as badly as I'd expected. However, I wanted to be overly dramatic, in order to make Jesse more nervous.

I clenched my teeth together. "Ouch, that really hurt," I grunted.

Jesse looked concerned. "You know, maybe I shouldn't do this. It's not my style, and besides, I don't think my mother would be too happy with me coming home with an ear pierced."

I rolled my eyes. "Don't chicken out now, you baby. We had a deal."

"I just... uh..." he hesitated. I softened.

"Jesse, trust me. You're going to be fine." I reached out and grabbed his hand, giving it what I hoped was a comforting squeeze. And was I imagining it, or did his eyes linger on mine for a moment too long?

But before I had time to think much about that, Jesse was in the chair and nervously gripping the armrests. The lady rubbed alcohol on his ear to disinfect it. "This won't hurt much," she said. "But if you scream or cry or both, we won't judge you."

I stifled a laugh and Jesse nodded uncertainly.

But when the lady raised her weird gun contraption to his ear, Jesse inhaled a deep breath and looked almost serene. He sure was good under pressure. Before he let the breath out, he had a stud in his ear.

Excitedly, I pulled the bucket list out of my purse and handed Jesse a pen. "I'll let you do the honors."

He took it and drew a large check mark in the box next to, "Get my cartilage pierced."

The rest of the day went by in a happy blur of stores and snacks, and by the time afternoon rolled by and we had to go, it felt like we'd only been at the mall for a few minutes. Nevertheless, we had to get on the road in order to get home in a timely matter, so we headed for the parking ramp.

I was actually surprised by how little we had bought. Jesse wasn't possession-oriented, and I was an extremely picky shopper, so despite the fact that we had both saved plenty of money to spend at the MOA, we didn't buy very much. I decided it was better that way though; my wallet had taken a bit of a hit that summer already.

On the way home, we practiced singing the song over and over and over and over and over again. Finally, we had it down well enough we could play it (on our air guitar or piano) and sing it without any hesitation.

"Now all we need to do is find an audience to perform it for," Jesse said after a particularly perfect run-through.

"And then we're done?" I pulled the list from my purse to reinspect it.

Jesse nodded solemnly, then flipped on the radio. "Might as well enjoy the last few hours." So with that, he began singing along loudly and purposefully off-key. I laughed and sang along with him, and the time and the miles seemed to fly by.

THE BUCKET LIST

When we pulled into my driveway, I was forlorn. The fact of the matter was, I wasn't sure what my life was going to look like once I no longer had the bucket list to consume my thoughts and my time. Would Jesse and I still be friends? Would I go back to constantly dwelling on Tate? Could I actually move on from this summer? But I tried to push those questions out of my mind as I got out of Jesse's car.

I forced a smile. "Thanks for coming with me. It was fun."

"Of course. I'll see you at work, alright?"

I nodded. "Yeah. See you."

- [x] Shop at the Mall of America
- [x] Write a song
- [x] Get my cartilage pierced

☐ SING IN FRONT OF A CROWD

The next day, I was dancing arou—I mean, sitting casually in my room listening to my iPod shuffle, when I heard a knock on the door. I made a mental joke that in five seconds Detective Harlem would barge in and start pointless interrogating me. I crack myself up.

However, when I opened the door, there were no police officers, detectives, or other authority figures, rather a tear-stained and red-faced Ella. "Ella? Hi, what's wrong?" I got no response. "Hey, come on up to my room." I made sure to look around to avoid any unwanted parental snooping. Luckily, neither my mother nor my father were in the general vicinity.

I shut the door to my room behind Ella, while she sat down on my bed. I took the swivel chair, then patiently waited for the news. I didn't even have to ask, Ella jumped right into it.

"Jesse just broke up with me..." she stated. Now, they'd only been dating a few weeks, and Ella wasn't like a crazy obsessed girlfriend, but she was a rather sensitive girl. I understood where she was coming from.

"Oh my God, Ella, I'm sorry. What did he say?"

"Well, I was over at his house and we were watching some crappy movie and then when it was over, I got up to get a glass of water and then he just sort of... said it. He wasn't mean about it or anything. I don't know... I thought we'd last a little longer than a few weeks. But he didn't say why."

What a jerk move: breaking up with her without explaining why.

Fury began bubbling up inside of me, but I didn't let it show. I sat with Ella up in my room and talked with her about it and tried to make her laugh, until she said she should get going.

On her way out, she paused in the doorway and said, "Hey, Leesie?"

"Yeah?"

"You're a good friend, you know that?"

I couldn't respond, so I just smiled as she closed the door. But my smile was dead the second she was gone.

I pulled my phone out of my pocket but stopped myself before dialling. This would have to be done in person.

I knocked angrily on the door, and gave Jesse a generous twelve seconds to open before knocking again, much harder.

Moments later, it swung open to reveal a confused looking Jesse. I immediately let myself into his house, and asked in a raised voice, "Why?"

"Why what?" he questioned.

"Why did you break up with Ella?"

He shut the door, and replied with a question of his own. "Why not?"

"Why not? Because she's awesome. She's pretty, she's sweet, and she's super easy to talk to. Now tell me Jesse: *why?!*"

Jesse said simply, "She isn't my type."

I scoffed. "Tell me something, Jesse. What was the real reason you showed up at my doorstep that first time? Was it really because you wanted someone to talk to about Tate's death?"

"I'm sorry, but if you're implying that I don't care about Tate, that's a direct offense to me and the friend I lost."

I wasn't able to respond for a moment, as I gathered my thoughts. "You know what I'm implying? I'm not saying you weren't buddies with Tate. I'm saying that maybe the bucket list is just some poetic excuse for you to hook up with me. Is that what it is to you?"

Jesse leaned in to emphasize his next words. "Absolutely not. Yes, I've always had a crush on you. But that's not the reason I went to Paris, to London, New York, Minnesota, and California."

I stared at him, trying to read his thoughts. "The reason I broke up with Ella has nothing to do with the bucket list. Nothing to do with Tate. I did it because I know you like me back."

I shook my head, tears beginning to well up in my eyes. "It doesn't matter, Jesse. And it never will." With that, I bolted out of his house, slamming the door behind me. I walked as quickly as possible, and I didn't look back.

It didn't matter. We didn't matter, because how could we? I ran home with tears streaming down my face, while darkness fell around me.

When I got home, I was thankful that my parents weren't around, so I wouldn't have to pass them to get to my room. They would've undoubtedly seen my tears, my stupid tears over some stupid boy and this stupid summer.

I threw myself onto my bed and buried my face in a pillow. I wanted to scream. This whole situation was a mess; Ella was heartbroken, Jesse was probably furious at me, and I was confused and distressed at the same time. How did we end up like this?

How could Jesse possibly be so completely and utterly idiotic? It was such a dumb idea to break up with Ella just because I might possibly maybe sometimes think I could like him. It's not like we'd ever work out; we were both leaving for college in a few weeks. Besides, it was our pasts that tied us together, not our futures. And I would not let myself get hurt by someone who wouldn't be a part of my future.

I lifted my head and looked across the room to where the bucket list was laying nonchalantly on my desk. It was at fault. It was false hope and fake absolution and now that it was ending, I could see that the mess it had promised to clean was bigger than ever.

Furiously, I got up and stampeded to the list. In absolute rage, I began tearing it to bits.

By the time the floor around me was littered with pieces of the list, I realized what a mistake I'd made. All of the hard work that Jesse and I (and even Ella) had put in to make those little checkmarks possible was down the drain. My hours and hours of work at a boring job making near-nothing were down the drain. The relationship I'd revived with Jesse was down the drain.

"I hate this!" I shouted and threw myself back onto my bed, sobbing uncontrollably. Every second of my miserable little existence had found its way to the floor. I missed Tate. I wasn't ready to be an adult. I didn't want the summer to be over. But it didn't matter. I wanted Ella to be happy. I wanted to move on. I wanted to be able to kiss Jesse without guilt seething in my gut. But it didn't matter. It didn't matter because Tate had made it impossible, and I was going to have to live with that forever.

His words came to my mind again. Not anything specific, just memories of things he'd said over the past few months. *May I have this dance?* "Shut up!" *It's because Leesie's the brave one.* "Shut up, Jesse!" *Suddenly this feels very real. The bucket list.* "You're damn well right it's real! Everything is real, and it'll never not be real! This will never be something I forget about! This is my life now, and it's *your* fault! *Your fault!*"

I abandoned myself to the sobs, and didn't regain control until several minutes later.

I looked back to the scattered pieces of the bucket list laying on my floor. How had I so easily knocked down what I had worked so hard to build? I picked up my phone and desperately searched for Jesse in my contacts. He would know what to do.

But when it rang and rang, and kept ringing, through the third and fourth call, I knew I had to give up. He wasn't answering. He was probably giving me the silent treatment. He'd probably realized I was a lost cause and couldn't be helped; I would be cold and guarded and afraid for the rest of my life.

*"Leesie, Mrs. Allen and I are going out tonight, and your father's staying late at work. How would you like to spend the night at Jesse's?"

Leesie began jumping up and down with excitement; it must be understood, a sleepover is the climax of luxury to a child. "I knew you'd be excited!" Leesie's mother smiled. "Oh, and Mrs. Roe said Jesse's best friend is going to be there too, so that'll be fun!" She then leaned to kiss her daughter on the forehead. "Pack a sleeping bag and some jammies, alright? Then I'll walk you down there."

As she closed the door, Leesie's face grew pale. She was incredibly shy, and didn't want to spend the night with a stranger. Who was this "best friend"? Would they be nice? And even though she did like Jesse, and his family, she'd never slept over there before.

However, Leesie was brave, and liked playing with friends, so she steeled herself and then proceeded to pack.

When Leesie and her mom arrived at Jesse's house, Leesie felt suddenly afraid. But in the end, she decided the fun of a sleepover was worth the scariness of meeting a new person.

Leesie threw her arms around her mother's waist. "Bye, Mommy." Then, she turned and knocked on Jesse's door, before she could lose her nerve.

Almost immediately, Jesse opened the door. He was covered in flour, and said excitedly, "We're making cookies! Want to help?"

"Oh... sure," Leesie responded, excited by the thought of cookies but otherwise reluctant. She stepped inside, placed her overnight bag on the stairway and got hit with a strong smell of vanilla.

"Jesse, I think I put too much vanilla in," a high voice called from the kitchen. Jesse ran through the archway that led to the Roe's massive kitchen, and Lessie hesitantly followed.

Once in the kitchen, she saw two metal bowls, a couple of containers filled with ingredients, and a small blonde girl with the bluest eyes Leesie had ever seen. "I put too much vanilla in..." she said, showing Jesse an empty vanilla extract bottle. "Now we have to make a new batch. Would that be okay, Mrs. Roe?"

Jesse's mom was in the dining room, building blocks with Jesse's little brother, Graham. She looked up and said, "I don't think we have any more vanilla. We could maybe go to the store to get some later, though."

"I think it'll be alright Tate. I love vanilla, especially vanilla ice cream." Jesse reassured.

"But it'll be *too* vanilla-y. It'll be gross!" she laughed.

"You could put in the opposite and balance it out," Leesie quietly suggested. They looked at her and giggled.

"Sure!" The girl exclaimed.

"Yeah!" Jesse chimed in. "Can we try it, Mom?"

"I suppose, but it might not work."

"That sounds delicious." The girl made an "mmm" sound as if she had already bitten into a warm, melty chocolate chip cookie.

"What's the opposite of vanilla?" Jesse asked seriously.

"Chocolate, dummy!" The girl laughed.

"Oh yum!" Jesse responded. "Leesie, come help me find some chocolate." Leesie couldn't help but smile; Jesse had picked her to help him.

Within the next few minutes, there were two bottles of chocolate syrup, a bag of chocolate chips, a few candy bars, and a container of chocolate icing out on the counter.

"How much do we put in?" the girl asked.

"All of it!" Leesie declared. The girl flashed her a toothy grin, and introduced herself.

"I'm Tate."

"I'm Leesie."

"Oh sorry; I forgot to introduce you guys," Jesse stated. But it didn't really matter, Tate and Leesie seemed to get along without any help.

An hour or so later, the timer beeped. Jesse's mom came to take the pan out and reveal a massive conglomeration of chocolate and dough. It smelled delicious, and was rich to even the craziest of chocolate lovers. The three children found it oddly delicious. They called it, "Swirly Cookie."

Later that evening, they were setting up to watch a movie in the living room when Tate said, "Will you be my friend Leesie? Me and Jesse are best friends and you could be our bestest friend too."

"Yeah, when we grow big we're going to get married!" Jesse said.

"And have ten kids!" Tate added.

"And live together forever and ever!"

"You could be our friend too, Leesie. Please?"

Leesie giggled and nodded her head. "I'll be your friend."

It'd been four days since I'd checked my phone. Four days since I'd even wanted to make contact with anyone. It's funny how time becomes meaningless when you're not going anywhere.

My parents were right back to worrying. I can't say I blame them, it must've seemed like I'd been doing so well recently. I was, I suppose. I wanted to move on; I really did. But it wasn't in my power to do that, and the people who might've been able to actually help me... well, I hadn't seen them in a week.

The second to last Sunday of the summer, I was dragged along by my mom to church. "Come on, Leesie, I think it will help you," she said while I involuntarily trudged out to the car.

During the service, I let my mind wander, and barely noticed anything the pastor said. I stood up when I was supposed to stand up, I sat down when I was supposed to sit down, but I didn't engage.

But by far the worst part going to church is the social hour after the service. And when they say hour, they mean hour, or maybe two, or maybe three, or maybe five hundred thousand. You know how moms get when they start chatting.

That particular time, I decided to give up and let my mom converse in peace for a while. I sat down in one of the plush armchairs near the entryway, and was just about to pull out my phone when I saw something interesting. Across the room, Brad Shager's mom was talking animatedly to the youth director, and standing beside them was none other than the jerky jock himself.

Brad was holding onto the hand of a little boy, who I could only assume was his little brother. The two boys looked nearly identical, except one was five and the other was eighteen. But Brad wasn't paying much attention the boy. He was looking sulkily around the room until he saw me, and our eyes locked.

For several moments, we were staring at each other. Brad was looking at me so intently it was as if he was trying to tell me something, like he wanted to communicate a message by gazing into my eyes.

Eventually, I couldn't take it anymore, so I got up and walked over to him.

"Hi, Leesie," he said, and the defeat in his tone was so intense I wanted to cry. His voice in that moment was the embodiment of what I was feeling. Maybe we did have something in common.

"Hey," I responded after a moment. "Sorry about the other day." I blushed remembering our encounter in the store.

"Ah, don't worry about it."

I nodded. We were both silent for a moment, while I stared down at Brad's little brother. "I've been wanting to ask you," I started after a few seconds' silence, "about if you know why Tate committed suicide."

"I, uh..." Brad stuttered awkwardly. "Tate and I were broken up before she, you know..." He glanced down at his brother, who looked completely clueless and yet as if he was hanging on Brad's every word. "We can talk about it some other time," he stated finally.

Ouch, rejection. Oh well. I could understand why Brad didn't want to talk about death and drugs in front of his brother, who couldn't have been older than six. "Okay," I agreed. "Some other time." But let's be honest, I didn't actually expect it to happen.

But it did happen. On Monday, I heard the doorbell, and a minute later, my mom called me downstairs.

I excitedly thundered down the steps, expecting to see Jesse. When I spotted Brad, I stopped in my tracks. "Hey, Leesie," he said, shifting his weight from foot to foot uncomfortably.

"Hi," I managed to sputter, continuing down the steps with hesitation.

My mom, awkwardly standing between us, decided it was a great time to leave. "Well, I'll be in the kitchen if you need anything." And with that, she scampered off.

A few seconds of pressing silence passed before Brad spoke again. "I was wondering if you'd like to go on a walk." He gestured to the door.

"Um, sure," I agreed, understanding it was a ploy to escape my mother's earshot.

Once we were outside, Brad said, "Sorry that I just showed up here."

"No, no, it's fine. I was just watching Dr. Who, and I'm sure the aliens can wait a bit." That got a smile out of him, even though it was a weak one.

"I wanted to talk to you about Tate. I would've at church, but Harry, my brother... I don't want him thinking about that stuff."

"Of course, I understand. I shouldn't have asked."

"No," he assured me firmly. "You deserve answers."

I nodded, but didn't say anything.

Finally, he continued, "She wasn't depressed when we were dating. It started after she broke up with me."

"She broke up with you because you cheated," I interjected quickly.

Ever so slowly, he nodded. "You've done your research. Don't know what you need me for."

I stopped, and sat down on the curb. Brad followed my lead. "What I really want to know about," I told him, "is the Ecstasy."

Brad's mouth fell open. "I thought you didn't know about that."

I stood up swiftly, and exclaimed accusingly, "Of course I didn't know about it! I actually cared about Tate. I would've done something: stopped her or told her parents or something."

"But her parents knew."

"What?" I blurted.

Brad picked at the grass in my neighbor's yard, and took his time before answering, "Her parents knew about the drugs. They found out, about a month before... you know. One night she randomly told me to meet her at the park, and she was crying, and she told me everything that happened. Maybe because I was the one who got her into that mess."

I stared at him for a moment. "What did her parents do?"

"They lost it. She told me that the night her dad came across the stash in her bedroom, her parents screamed at her and cried and practically disowned her. And they never changed from that point on. She was shunned. She told me that was the second worst night of her life."

"What was the first?" I pressed, even though I was scared to hear the response.

"I asked her that too. She said, 'Tonight, because I know what I have to do now.' And when I asked her what that was, she wouldn't say. So I switched tactics, and asked her why she had to do it."

"Are you out of your mind?!" I exclaimed. "Why didn't you tell anyone what she was going to do?"

He bit his lip, the guilt evident on his face. "Listen, Leesie, I didn't think... I never imagined it would be something like that. I thought she was going to run away or something."

I rolled my eyes. "Oh, well that's fine then."

"Can I just finish telling you the story?"

"Alright," I muttered.

"So, I asked why. Then she said she had to do it because she didn't feel anything for anyone anymore, except one person: you. And she told me that she was very sorry for everything she's put you through."

I felt my eyes sting, but no tears. "She didn't even have the courage to tell me herself." I shook my head.

Brad didn't know what to say. There probably wasn't anything for him to say.

After a minute or two of silence, I stood up and walked away, giving only a quiet, "See you," as a goodbye. He gave a small wave in response, and after that, I never saw him again.

Right after Tate died, I kept looking for someone, anyone really, to incriminate for what happened. But now, right when I had people to accuse, I decided assigning blame was pointless. It wouldn't bring her back. There wasn't anything in the world I wanted more than that, but if it wasn't going to happen, I wasn't going to try to make it happen.

That afternoon, I was sitting at my desk, browsing Pinterest, but my mind was wandering elsewhere. I was thinking about the way Brad didn't tell anyone what Tate was going to do. I knew I should've been furious, but oddly, I wasn't mad at all.

A small notification came up in the bottom-lefthand corner of my computer screen, telling me I had received an email from a jluarez@gmail.com.

Hello Leesie.

First and foremost I would like to apologize for the way I acted at our last session. I hope that you do not hold my moment of weakness against me, or think too badly of me. You see, for the longest time I was blaming myself for Tate's death. I thought I should've been able to stop it, or at least know it was coming. But I've recently come to a realization.

I once told you that a conversation is like a road. I am a big fan of metaphor, and I think everyone should be; metaphors can help us understand concepts that would otherwise be incomprehensible. So I would like to bring up another metaphor.

Tate was a war. The tragic ending to her life, a battlefield. And I'm afraid, Leesie, that there have been many, many casualties. Tate's closest friends, her family, and even those who barely knew her were left to fight her battles because she couldn't handle them any longer. You and I have been breaking under the burden of suffering that she's left us with.

But here's the secret: it doesn't have to be that way. We don't have to fight her war. All we have to do is struggle long enough to escape. So don't give up hope, Leesie. You're already nearly out.

I hope I'll get to see you again someday. I'm sorry I didn't do a very good job as your therapist.

-Jenni (Dr. Señuarez)

After reading it, I shut my laptop, unsure what to feel. Part of me was insulted; was Tate's life nothing more than a war? Was I just a casualty? A statistic waiting to be counted?

But a bigger part of me couldn't help but agree. I was breaking under the weight of the grief Tate had left me with, and most days, her death did feel like a battle in a tragic war. So maybe Jenni was right about the other part too. Maybe I could escape, maybe I was already halfway out.

I stared across the room at my phone, which I'd completely ignored for over a week. I couldn't bring myself to pick it up though, because chances were no one had bothered to text or call me, and that was depressing.

I couldn't imagine what Jesse was thinking about me. I'd told him that his feelings didn't matter right to his face, then said mine didn't either. But it was true, and as long as Tate had a grip on my heart it would stay that way.

But despite her unclenching grip, something inside me said that things would only get worse the longer I put off picking up my phone. So I just did it.

"One new message from Jess!"

One text... better than none, I suppose. I opened it up and saw he'd sent it yesterday morning.

Jess: *I'm sorry, Leesie. I really am. And I want to show you something. Go downtown tomorrow, at three. Meet at the bean.*

I checked my watch: 2:30. I had thirty minutes to arrive at my last chance. This was the final window, the final opportunity I had to save my friendship with Jesse. So of course I took it.

I stuffed the bag that held the remains of the bucket list into my pocket, with the hopes that I could get Jesse to forgive me for tearing it up. Then, I ran downstairs, grabbed the keys and yelled to my parents that I was heading to Chicago.

"Why?" My mom shouted back, but I didn't have time to explain.

"I'll tell you later, I'm going to be late!" I shouted as I shut the door behind me. I had my fingers crossed that she wouldn't get mad about my sudden, unexplained departure.

Driving down the highway, I could barely breathe. My nerves were all over the place. What if I was too late, and Jesse had already left? I sped up a bit, and moved to the left lane.

When I finally arrived in Chicago, found parking, and jogged to The Bean, it was already 3:14.

"Crap," I said under my breath. I'd probably missed him. But glancing around, I spotted him, and muttered, "Crap," once more. He was playing his guitar and singing near The Bean, and he had a keyboard beside him. There was a small crowd gathered in front of him, and it looked like they were generally enjoying it. I won't lie, Jesse has a nice voice.

I tried not to think about the keyboard and the nervousness I was feeling while I listened to Jesse sing. He was playing "Back Home" by Andy Grammer, one of Tate's all-time favorite songs. I clapped along with the rest of the audience, keeping the beat.

Jesse looked up and saw me for the first time. He smiled. I smiled.

When the song ended, Jesse paused and set his guitar down on the bench of the keyboard. Then he gestured for me to come stand next to him. I reluctantly obeyed, all too aware of the many eyes of the audience on me.

Then he looked back out at the gathering crowd and spoke.

"Now, the real reason I came here this afternoon." He crouched and rummaged through his guitar case for a few seconds, emerging with a small photo. He stood up and held it out for everyone to see. It was a picture of a smiling Tate. A happy Tate.

I was hit with a wave of grief. Jesse continued, "This girl committed suicide about four months ago. We," Jesse looked at me, then back to the crowd, "are her friends. Were her friends." Suddenly, I felt his hand around mine. "So today," I could feel him squeeze my hand before finishing, "we sing to her."

I stared at him, in a state of shock and growing nervousness. I hadn't been expecting to sing in front of a crowd today, but I guess Jesse had been. "After you," he whispered, quiet enough so only I could hear, then gestured to the keyboard.

Feeling as though my legs were made of lead, I slowly walked over to the keyboard and sat down. On the music stand was a printed copy of the chords and lyrics Jesse and I had written while driving to and from Minnesota. I felt my hands shake, and wished I had been more diligent with my piano practicing.

I started playing the piano entrance, relatively competently, considering my lack of recent practice. It sounded almost like a real piece. When I started singing the first verse, I forgot that the crowd was there. That was the first and last time I had ever sung the song and felt what it was, what it meant. It's meaning was so... heavy. It was the final goodbye to the bucket list, to everything we'd done, and mostly to Tate. With each note, a different memory of the summer flashed through my thoughts.

California drove by. Europe flew above us. The Mall of America stood in the crowd. That day that Jesse first knocked on my door came to mind, and it brought a lump to my throat with it. Sitting there, performing, was truly the end of the end. I thought of the tree house, and Ella, and working hours upon hours at Hollister. Despite being the worst summer of my life, I couldn't ignore all the goodness and all the friendship that came to me when I was left behind.

While I was singing the last verse of the song, I looked out into the crowd, realizing for the first time that they were watching intently. Standing in the back, a lady in her sixties was tearing up, and next to her a man I assumed to be her husband was looking toward the sky.

And then it was over. When I hit the last note, the crowd clapped ferociously. Before Jesse had the chance to set down his guitar, a lady walked up and tried to hand him a dollar. He rejected it by saying, "No, no; I'm freelance."

As the crowd began to disperse, and we were packing up the gear, Jesse turned to me and said, "Well, I guess you can cross that off the bucket list."

"Oh my gosh!" I responded, in distress, as I suddenly remembered my ripping rampage. "I'm so sorry, Jesse."

"What?" he asked cluelessly.

I dug around in my purse and pulled out the small baggie holding the remnants of the list.

Slowly, Jesse took it from my hand and looked down and the shreds with a crestfallen expression painted on his face. But after a moment he smiled weakly, and assured me, "I probably would've done this a long time ago if I'd had it with me constantly. It hasn't been easy."

I let out a sigh of relief; at least Jesse wasn't furious with me, even if I was with myself.

"Can I take this home for a while?"

I shrugged. "Sure. It's just scraps now."

Jesse changed the subject. "Will you go somewhere with me tomorrow? Say, around ten?"

"Where?"

A sneaky smile snuck onto his face. "That's a secret."

- ☑ Sing in front of a crowd
- ☑ Complete everything on my bucket list

When I walked into my house, my parents were suddenly on either side of me. My dad informed me excitedly, "Leese, we saw you on the news!"

"What?!"

My parents then proceeded to show me a shaky video my mom had taken on her phone. Despite my parents' loud commentary in the background, I could see and kind of hear a short news report about two Batavia Lake teenagers who had sung a song to their deceased friend.

After watching the video, I talked with my parents a bit about it, then rushed up to my room.

I decided I should talk to Ella. I hadn't heard from her since she was upset over Jesse, and I wanted to make sure she was okay. So I texted her.

Me: *Hey Ella. How are you?*

Ella: *I'm better now, I think.*

Me: *That's great!*

Ella: *Hey, saw you on the news. That was amazing!*

Me: *Thanks! It was the last thing on the list, so we're all done!*

Ella: *She would've loved it Leesie.*

Me: *Why do you think?*

Ella: *Even after everything she's done to you, you showed that you still loved her. It takes a special kind of friendship to give a gift that's not deserved.*

I waited a moment before responding, fighting back a bittersweet smile.

Me: *Ella, I just wanted to say that I'm glad it was you. I'm glad you were the one who told me.*

Ella: *That's what friends are for, Leesie.*

The next day, Jesse pulled up to my house at exactly ten o'clock. By that point in our relationship, I was used to his unusual promptness, so I was watching for him through the window. When I walked outside, he held up the somehow intact bucket list behind the windshield, grinning. He rolled down the window and stated, "Nothing duct tape can't fix."

I hopped into the car, and instantly began badgering him, "So, where are we going?"

"It's a secret, I told you."

"A surprise party?" I asked hopefully.

"No, unfortunately, you won't like it nearly that much. But I think it's important."

My hopes fell, and they seemed to settle as a dull weight somewhere in my stomach. "Well, that's great."

As we drove across town, I began to grow more and more suspicious. Why would he be taking me somewhere secret that I wouldn't like? He'd probably assumed I wouldn't have agreed to go. But if it was so important, I would've agreed, right?

My over-analyzation didn't get to run free for long, however, because we soon pulled into the parking lot of the graveyard. "We're going to the graveyard?" I questioned critically.

"Like I said, you might not enjoy it, but I think it's important."

"Jesse, seriously? I'm fine. I went to the funeral and said goodbye already."

"But you haven't even seen the grave." He turned in his seat and put a hand on my shoulder. "Leesie, please?" His voice was so tender, so sincere. I bit my lip and reluctantly nodded, then got out of the car before I could change my mind.

I felt nervous. I didn't want to see her grave, but I had to do it, for Jesse. I owed him that much after everything I had put him through.

He walked around the car and stood next to me for a moment, both of us looking out at the hills full of headstones. It was odd to think that each one of those meant something so significant to certain people, but to me they were each just another rock in a field of hundreds.

After a moment, Jesse looked over at me, then grabbed my hand and laced his fingers through mine. The thought didn't even occur to me to let go. As he led me up the path, I tried my hardest to keep my mind off of where we were going. I tried to focus on other things, like the knobbly roots of an ancient-looking tree, or the number of petals on a particular flower.

But before long, we stopped in front of a small grey headstone with the simple engraving, "Tate Jordyn Conscivit."

I knelt down, letting go of Jesse's hand, and traced the letters of her name with my fingers. The stone felt hot, and the air felt hot, and my tears felt hot.

Slowly, I stood back up and took Jesse's hand again. After a moment, I decided it was okay for me to rest my head on his shoulder, so I did. Tears ran down my cheek and got soaked up in his tee shirt.

"Remember Swirly Cookie, Jess?" I asked quietly.

"Yeah." We stayed silent after that, remembering simply everything about the past.

"I'm so mad at her," I whispered at last.

"Me too," he responded, and I could feel his jaw moving against the top of my head.

A few seconds of silence passed, before I added, "I wish I wasn't."

"Me too," Jesse said again.

Suddenly, I felt felt a surge of rage. I fell to my knees once again, and slammed the ground with my fist. "Why wasn't I good enough for you?!" I shouted, even though I knew she couldn't hear me. All at once, my tears turned into sobs and my sadness turned into despair. My body was shaking uncontrollably and I could hardly catch my breath. I was just so sad, so mad.

Jesse knelt down beside me, and looked into my eyes. "Why did she want to leave us?" I asked him weakly, feeling the burning red of my face.

"I don't know, Leesie," he answered, and I realized there were tears in his eyes too. "I don't know." I turned back to the grave, closing my eyes and letting my head fall to the ground as more tears poured out.

Jesse put a hand on my back, and I turned to him and threw myself into his arms. I hugged him so tightly, with all my strength and will. "Let's go home," he whispered into my ear. I nodded.

The drive home was dead silent. It wasn't an awkward silence, it was a silence filled with relief. Nothing was said because nothing needed to be said. But, when we arrived at my house, I waited to get out of the car, gathering my thoughts.

Without looking at Jesse, I began, "I know it doesn't matter." His head turned to mine, puzzlement filling his expression. I faced him, knowing that what I was about to say had been something I'd needed to say for the longest time. "But I wish it did."

Then I opened the door, got out, and started walking slowly toward my house. I turned back in time to see Jesse smile the tiniest smile, then drive away. I took a deep breath as the sticky summer air turned into a crisp autumn breeze. Walking up to my front door, I felt a hundred pounds lighter with each step. And I never looked back again.

The faint light of dusk was still seeping through my partially opened blinds onto my hardwood desk. On the desk sat the purple pom-pom pen and the same piece of notebook paper from the beginning of summer, still without a single word on it. I sighed and picked up the pen, and put its tip to the paper. For just a moment, I

THE BUCKET LIST

paused. Then, in the neatest handwriting I could manage, at the very top of the once-empty page, I wrote, "Leesie's Bucket List."

Made in the USA
Lexington, KY
31 May 2018